Stepping into the Light

CANDEE FICK

DEDICATION

To all those who believe in fairy tales…
But don't feel like royalty.

This castle series is for you.

GLOSSARY OF SCOTTISH TERMS

Bailey - inner courtyard separating the outer fortified wall of the castle complex from the main building housing the leader's family.

Bairn - a child

Canna - can not

Confessor - a priest who hears confessions and gives absolution and spiritual counsel

Curtain wall - external fortified wall surrounding a medieval castle complex. Often also surrounded by a moat.

Dinna - did not

Donna - do not

Fortnight - a period of two weeks

Friar - a member of a mendicant religious order. Called "brother" and wore long robes made of wool with a rope belt around the waist. Took vows of poverty, chastity, and obedience but typically traveled around serving an area rather than remaining cloistered like monks

Ken - know

Keep - the castle itself or the multistory home for the ruling family that also contained a great hall and often sleeping quarters for the soldiers

Laird - Similar to "Lord," a term of respect when addressing or referring to the clan leader

Loch - lake

Mayhap - perhaps

Midsummer's Eve - The longest day of the year (around the 23rd or 24th of June). Originally celebrated as a Celtic fire festival to bless the crops and beasts but later coincided with the Feast of St. John the Baptist to celebrate his birthday. Since it fell between the planting and harvesting seasons, it was a time to relax and became the traditional month for weddings as well

Palfrey - a docile horse used for ordinary riding as opposed to a warrior's steed

Pasty - a folded pastry case with a savory filling, typically of seasoned meat and vegetables

Plaid - woven wool fabric that was used as a blanket and also worn over a woman's gown or in place of a man's trousers (in the later fashion of a kilt), usually woven with distinctive colors or patterns to differentiate one clan from another

Saffron - an orange-yellow flavoring, food coloring, and dye made from the dried stigmas of a crocus

Sennight - one week

Score - twenty years. A half score would be ten years, so a half score and three would be the same as thirteen

Tankard - a tall beer mug

Tartan - see "plaid" above

Verra - very.

PROLOGUE

1412 ~ Scottish Highlands

Alone at last, Moira Gunn collapsed onto her knees in the middle of the glade.

Chest heaving from her dash away from the castle, she sat back onto her heels and inhaled the pine-scented air. Today it might take more than her favorite hideaway to restore her peace.

She dried her tears with the edge of the Gunn clan's woolen plaid draped around her slight frame then studied her surroundings. Ears keen to a rustling in the nearby underbrush, Moira placed a hand over her throat where her breath lodged in fear. Her heart pounded as the peace around her shattered.

A flash of red through the branches confirmed her worst fears moments before Devlin, the captain of Isla's personal guard, pushed through the undergrowth into the clearing. The laird's wife insisted on the unique shirt color as proof of their authority, but the deep hue made the ruffians easier to spot throughout the forested countryside…and avoid in times of trouble.

Until today.

"Look who I found outside the castle gates." Devlin sneered at Moira from a stone's toss away. "Thought ye could sneak out, did ye?"

Mayhap there was naught to fear but another tongue-lashing. Still, Moira eased from the grass to her feet, prepared to bluff her way out of the danger prickling the back of her neck.

Either that or run.

Except even with scattered thickets and patches of brambles, the stretch of forest between the castle wall and the nearby ravine wouldna hide her for long.

Devlin took a step closer. "Lady Isla sent ye to the kitchens for a reason."

'Twas punishment for ruining her gown as they broke their fast that morn, except 'twasna her fault. Ilsa's spoiled son Roan had smeared the fruit tart onto Moira's skirt then stood by with nary a word—though smirking—whilst Moira shouldered the blame.

"But I didna…" Her voice trailed off with resignation. Her father's new wife never believed her, and lately she'd spent more time away from her family than with them.

"Ye were sent to prepare the meal for yer clan." Devlin crossed bulging arms across his chest, an angry scowl marring his face.

Moira side-stepped a patch of multicolored flowers to put more distance between them. She might have been happy helping in the kitchens, but the cook had complained she was underfoot and didna belong there.

Didna seem she belonged anywhere.

Especially by her father's side.

A sob caught in her throat. The whole clan had been abuzz for days with speculation about their laird's mysterious illness until she simply couldn't face another moment of the gossip feeding her fears.

What would she do if he died? Who would protect her then?

Members of their clan came to offer their herbal cures and pay their respects to their laird, yet she wasna even allowed to sing for him like she had many times before.

Still, a lass should be allowed to greet her father on her birthday—especially her thirteenth, when she officially moved from bairn to maiden.

She fingered the jeweled brooch hanging from a leather cord around her neck. Her birthday gift three years ago while her mother was still alive.

Today held no gifts, only a heavy cloud.

The verra reason she'd sought the neglected side gate in the curtain wall and slipped away to rail at the injustice her life had become.

When Father Tomas returned from the Sinclair holding she would ask him why good people died. And why God seemed so far away.

A twig snapped in warning.

Too late. Moira had gotten distracted by her musings and dropped her guard.

In three quick steps, Devlin reached her side, and a hand snaked out to wrap around the plaited hair hanging down her back. "Don't ya ken? It be dangerous for a lass to be alone in the woods."

Panic coursed through her veins, and she struggled against the tightening grip that anchored her in place. "Let me go. My da will hear of this and—"

"He won't be causing any more trouble. And neither will ye." Devlin laughed, his foul breath hot on her face. "And ye won't be needin' this anymore." With a vicious jerk, he ripped away her precious heirloom.

The burning fire around her throat mirrored the agonizing void in her heart. "My mother's brooch—"

"Not anymore." He waved his dagger before her eyes. "There's only room for one pretty lady at this keep."

Icy dread settled into her stomach at the sight of the sharp blade. "Please. I'm just a lass." She twisted her head from side to side but could not break free of his hold on her hair.

Was he here out of some sort of misguided loyalty? Or jealousy on behalf of his mistress?

Heaven help her if he meant to scar her for life.

A brutal yank on her hair sent her spinning. He released her for an instant, but before she could gather her wits, she found herself facing the clearing but trapped against his body, anchored in place by a meaty hand on her forehead.

"Yer the one he's calling for in his fevered sleep." His dagger once again danced before her eyes. "All he can say is 'Mor.'"

Her heart ached at the drawn-out—cruel—imitation of a suffering man's delirium, then stopped as recognition dawned.

"Mor. Mor." The traitorous guard's mocking laughter rang out through the clearing as cold metal trailed down her cheek.

Moira's knees weakened at the sound of her dear mother's name. The mother who'd died in childbirth followed a few days later by her infant son. Would they all soon be reunited in the hereafter?

"Well, no more." The blade came to rest beneath her chin.

Lightheaded with fear, her knees buckled and she found herself falling, slipping from his grasp even as the blade pierced her neck, then sliced up the right side of her face with agonizing heat.

Harsh reality silenced her scream. With the knife at her throat, he had truly meant to kill her.

Only God could help her now.

A surge of unexpected strength sent her rolling to her right, then scrambling to her feet before running without direction into the woods. The crashing of feet behind her drove her farther from the safety of home and slightly downhill toward the distant rush of water as she darted one way then the other around trees.

Despite the hand pressed against her face, every step jarred her injury, sending more blood trickling through her fingers and down her arm. Still running, she risked a glance over her shoulder at her assailant. Devlin gained on her, fury twisting his features and the bloody dagger still in his hand.

Oh, dear God above, save me.

Moira ducked down, then rounded a cluster of tall bushes looking for a hiding place. Except she was closer to the ravine than she'd thought and the ground fell away beneath her feet. Pebbles and brush gouged her skin as she tumbled down the steep embankment. Every twist and turn against the rock-strewn wall of the ravine jarred her insides with the force of an axe chopping into a tree trunk. After a final rolling catapult off a large boulder, she landed on her back near the creek. Gasping like a fish on dry land, she lay still and fought to draw air into her lungs.

Above her came a bellow of outrage that reminded her to stay quiet—and motionless—in case Devlin could not already see her broken body at the bottom of the ravine.

A moment later, the vice-like grip around her chest eased enough for her to breathe again. Just in time for every bruise and scrape acquired during her fall to raise their voices in protest, joining the pulsing agony from her face and neck. Risking detection as Devlin stomped overhead, she lifted weak hands to hold the slashed flesh together, and then bit back a whimper at the renewed throbbing that brought tears to her eyes.

"When I find ye, ye'll wish ye were already dead."

Death might be welcome considering the misery of the moment. Then again, her father had always told her to be a brave lass because Gunns never quit.

A deep growl in the brush above her 'twas followed by a howl that sent chills up her already battered spine. A wolf. Somehow, either Devlin's actions or the scent of her blood had attracted the animal's attention.

The guard's war cry split through the air, and soon the sounds of battle between man and beast faded further away.

Thank Heaven for the distraction—except that the rest of the pack might be nearby.

Moira pushed the remaining dizziness away and eyed a nearby cluster of purple-hued bell heather. A half hour ago she would have relished the simple beauty of the flowering blooms and soaked in the happy twittering of lapwings in the branches overhead.

Now, if she didna wish to die when Devlin returned, she must get away.

She staggered to her feet and stumbled along the creek bed toward the loch. *Just...a little...farther.* Stepping over tree roots and around scrub brushes, Moira battled to remain upright even as her body weakened from the loss of blood.

From her periphery an elderly man with a wooden cart emerged. And then, she saw nothing at all.

CHAPTER ONE

Five years later...

E van Sinclair dragged a piece of bread through the meat
juices remaining on his trencher as he studied the
messenger being escorted across the rush-strewn great hall.
The height of the two guards flanking his sides overshadowed
the fair-haired young man, but that didn't stop his wide-eyed
inspection of the Sinclair holding and the number of men
gathered for the evening meal.

From his position at the end of the head table, Evan
caught his father's soldiers' whispered murmurs as the young
man, dressed in a blue plaid over a red tunic, passed them.
While most highlanders used saffron dye for their shirts, 'twas
apparent the Gunn clan chose to be different. And different
wasn't necessarily a good thing.

The messenger stopped a stone's throw away and pulled
a piece of rolled parchment from the pouch hanging from his
belt while waiting for the Sinclair laird to acknowledge his
presence. Evan watched his elder brother Donald, heir to the
lairdship and the most sought-after young man in the clan,
wave the man forward.

With no hesitation the messenger complied. "My Lady
Isla sends her kind regards and grateful reply." Mayhap his

averted gaze meant to be respectful, but the ironic twist of the man's lips belied his words.

Evan could only imagine the woman's initial reaction to his father's demand that the Gunn holding be absorbed into the vast Sinclair territory if an alliance were to be formed. The Sinclair men would scoff at such weakness, but only the truly desperate would agree to give up their identity and historic lands.

One of the escorting soldiers took the message and handed it to Evan's father, who immediately broke the seal and unrolled the parchment. As the laird read the message by the light of the fire behind him, Donald waved the messenger away with orders for the man to be fed before he departed. His behavior bespoke that of a man who believed himself to be in a position higher than he ranked, almost as if Donald were already laird in their father's place. Except no one would dare suggest that Finlay Sinclair should step down in his prime—even if his eldest son was prepared to lead.

The usual noise in the hall rose with voiced speculations over the content of the message. Some mocked the Gunns' weakness to seek an alliance while others brought up the reminder of the death of Isla's son. Without an obvious heir to lead them, the clan was vulnerable to attack and needed protection, especially since their home lay between two larger rival clans—the Sinclairs and the hated Sutherlands.

Like Donald, curiosity to sneak a peek at the words pulled Evan in his father's direction, but his mother's empty chair still stood in the way.

As it had for the two years since she had succumbed to a wasting disease.

A familiar ache of loss surfaced as he observed the empty chair, the noises from the hall drowned in another memory of his mother asking him about his day. She'd always remembered to ask. No one else understood what it was like to live in his brother's shadow.

But if the women of the clan had their way now that the mourning period for his lost mother had passed, a new mistress might claim the chair for herself. One whose interest might have little to do with the Sinclair clan as a whole but only her personal gain.

If only he could sit with the rest of the soldiers. But in the defined hierarchy of their training regiment, he would be seated halfway across the hall—and his father would never approve of his son sitting in that embarrassing position, at least during their meals.

The training grounds were another story.

"At least the Gunns didn't try to make an alliance with the Sutherlands." Evan's attention returned to the present as the man sitting at the adjacent table spat into the rushes covering the floor and his friends did the same at the sound of their enemy's name.

The seasoned warrior across the table grunted his approval. "I love a skirmish as much as the next lad, but the last thing we need is those unscrupulous brigands closer to our borders."

"Only because yer wife be carrying yer bairn."

Talk shifted to teasing the soon-to-be father for becoming soft, but Evan's mind backtracked to the initial comment. How did they know for sure that the Gunns hadn't reached out to the Sutherlands as well? What if Lady Isla played one clan leader against the other in order to distract— and weaken—the clans surrounding her borders? Except inciting such conflict could only lead to a war waged on the Gunn lands that would destroy her villages and farmland.

Only a fool would try such a thing, but still... Finlay Sinclair was too bold and confident a warrior to consider such a possibility and could very well walk into a trap. Not that he would listen to his youngest son if Evan ever were to suggest the possibility that they exercise caution.

His father chose that moment to push back from the table, then stood. "Well, me lads, I've got good news...and better news." His booming voice echoed through the hall and silenced all other conversation as his loyal men leaned in.

Even the servants stopped their duties for the grand announcement.

"After further consideration, Isla Gunn has accepted my terms and states that wedding preparations are already underway to seal our alliance at Midsummer's Eve in a fortnight." He grinned, then glanced at the parchment while resting one beefy hand on Donald's shoulder. "Says she's looking forward to seeing me and me son and…" His father's voice rose to a mocking feminine pitch. "…making our acquaintance."

The hall erupted with ribald jokes about a bride and groom becoming acquainted.

Despite having no desire to be bartered off into an arranged marriage for the sake of an alliance, Evan's stomach churned with the sour reminder that once again he'd been overlooked in Lady Isla's letter. As if only the firstborn mattered. As if only his brother could make a difference in the family.

"We'll leave in a sennight to make the journey, but that's not all." His father's shoulders shook with laughter as he eyed the message again. "She's taken it upon herself to gather all of the eligible maidens and widows from the clan for us to select from. And she isn't opposed to multiple alliances between the clans to form a stronger bond." If the gleam in his father's eye meant anything, Evan truly might end up with a stepmother out of the bargain.

More laughter rippled throughout the hall, including jokes from men eager to see the Gunn maidens and seek out those alliances.

Just not any of the permanent kind.

Evan frowned and pushed aside the remnants of his meal. Such talk might be the way of men, but it would never have been spoken were his mother still alive.

Nearby, his father returned to his seat and beckoned the scribe to prepare a reply. As the man hurried over with his wooden box of writing materials, the Sinclair laird leaned closer to his eldest son with clear instructions to find a prize in the bunch, settle down, and secure the family line with an heir.

As if already having a second son in the family wasn't enough.

Brushing aside the latest reminder of his insignificance, Evan reached for his goblet of ale. Perhaps it was time to build a life of his own and find a bride. Someone who truly cared about him.

He shook his head. Nay. All the lasses here had their sights set on Donald. Except after his brother married a Gunn, they might be willing to settle for second best.

He swallowed the ale and his bitter thoughts, then tried to join the others in their glee at the thought of new pretty lasses who would strengthen their clan with fresh bloodlines. After a minute, the topic grew dull and he glanced around the hall, seeking a new distraction.

Across the way, he spotted their resident priest talking to the Gunn messenger. Father Tomas used to also spend time with the other clan before Lady Isla had banned him from the Gunn land, desiring instead her own confessor nearby to aid in her grief over losing her second husband. The priest gave the sign of the cross and a smothering sense of foreboding settled over Evan's heart.

Something about this whole situation wasn't right.

But Heaven help him if he approached his father with nothing more than another of his intuitions. He needed proof and trusted only himself to uncover the truth and put these senseless fears to rest.

Come daybreak he could easily slip away from the castle and journey across the border onto Gunn land. While there, he would learn firsthand whether or not their girls were of the pretty variety and gather information to help his father make the right decision about joining the Sinclair and Gunn clans. And along the way, mayhap he could prove second sons were just as worthy as firstborn ones.

Depending on how long it took to ease his worries about the alliance, he could be back before the rest of the group left. Or slip in among them along the way since they never seemed to notice his presence—or absence—anyway.

Welcomed or not, Evan would do what he could to protect his family.

CHAPTER TWO

"Maggie, lass." The shoemaker raised his voice to be heard above the nooning crowd at the Kilglashan Inn.

Moira glanced his direction and smoothed the skirt of the simple gown beneath her plaid. After five years, she still had trouble answering to her assumed name.

"Fetch me more ale while I wait for me pasty. I'm yet half asleep." The shoemaker yawned so wide that she feared he'd break his jaw. "Our new bairn is yet keepin' us up at night."

She snatched the pitcher and hastened over to refill his tankard and those of a few other men nearby. The task would have been easier without the cloud of dark red hair hanging loose around her face, but 'twas simpler to cover her scars than open herself to even more ridicule. Or worse yet, discovery.

Situated along the seldom-used road leading to their border with the Sinclair clan, the inn was frequented by merchants from the nearby village. In fact, with the exception of the traveling friar in the corner of the room, all of these men had seen her before. But that didn't stop them from staring.

If only she could hide out in the kitchens like she usually did. Or at least stay at the fringes of the main room rather than wade into the midst of the talkative villagers. However, with their regular serving girl on her way to the Gunn keep to be considered for the marriage alliance, Moira had been forced from her kitchen refuge into the main room where she was subject to scrutiny

She raised her eyes from the pitcher of ale and spotted Graham, the innkeeper, across the room deep in conversation with one of the local farmers who supplied their barley. He spent more time talking than serving given his role at the inn, but she could forgive him that much. He was, after all, still the hero who had looked out for her ever since she'd stumbled upon him and his cart.

After replacing the pitcher atop the oak barrel of ale, Moira slipped into the kitchen. "Ma, we've orders for three more pasties and a bowl of stew."

"I just pulled another pan from the oven." Lavena, Graham's dear wife who had nursed Moira back to health, waved a hand at the table where a row of steaming meat pies cooled, then resumed stirring the pot of simmering barley malt. "And while the stew ye started has been a simmerin' all morning, methinks it needs yer special Maggie touch."

A sniff of the air had Moira reaching for her spice jars. Without even a taste, she could tell exactly what it needed to keep the customers coming back. She stirred a few pinches of seasoning into the stew, tasted the broth, and handed the ladle to Lavena, whose gnarled fingers crooked over the cutlery.

Moira bit her bottom lip, the weight of her worry settling on her chest. Her stew needed to do more than keep customers returning to the inn—it needed to keep her adoptive parents in business with a leak-free roof over their heads. With the couple aging more every year, where would she live once they were gone? What would she do then?

A smile creased Lavena's wrinkled face. "Now 'tis perfect."

16

Moira ladled stew into a wooden bowl, then gathered the other orders before returning to the main room in time to catch the tanner's report about his trip to the Gunn keep earlier in the week. While delivering the food and taking orders from a couple of newcomers, she listened to the latest news from home and the preparation for the Midsummer's Eve celebration.

"Strange things have been happening to the marriageable maidens…" The tanner's eyes widened as those around him leaned forward for more of the tale. Graham elbowed between two of his friends to hear the gossip firsthand.

"Which maidens?" Beside him, the lanky cooper took a large bite of his pasty, then swiped the back of his hand over his mouth, dislodging crumbs that fell onto the wooden table.

The tanner eyed the men at his table, then lifted his gaze to the other eavesdropping villagers. "The ones Isla summoned to the castle for beauty treatments and lessons to improve their manners so they're more likely to be chosen by the Sinclair laird."

Laughter broke out around the room along with a few comments about the Gunn men benefitting from the leftover maidens once the merge was done.

Typical men. Moira hid her rolling eyes behind the screen of hair, though her fingers inched upward to the puckered gash splitting the right side of her face. At least she would be spared the danger of being summoned to the castle. No one would want a disfigured bride.

When the joking about pretty girls died down, the miller leaned around his neighbor to ask the question on Moira's mind. "But despite my pleas, my Sheena insisted on going. What's happening to the girls who go to the castle?"

Moira's stomach soured at the thought the inn's former serving girl might be in danger.

The tanner frowned. "Mysterious illness. Accidental cuts. Falls down the stairs. I traveled a bit with one family who was there to collect their injured daughter since she was no longer considered worthy of consideration. The girl herself refused to speak of what had happened within the castle gates."

A hush of disquiet settled over the room and one man reached out to squeeze the miller's shoulder. The tanner lowered his voice as he continued. "'Twas even a story of a girl pitching into the fire. She supposedly suffered burns on her face and arms, then was sent away without benefit of a healer."

The cooper cleared his throat and glanced at the miller. "Sorry, Tristan, but I'm a thinkin' they aren't accidents. It wouldn't surprise me to learn Isla is eliminating the competition so she can marry another laird herself."

Several of the men crossed themselves even as they agreed with the horrifying possibility that their leader would deliberately hurt members of the clan for personal gain.

A chill ran up her spine. Such fears were more than a mere possibility.

Moira gathered a few empty dishes, eager to distance herself from more gossip about soldiers being sent further afield to gather more girls. As she turned away from the table, one newcomer reached out and pulled her onto his lap, his mouth descending as if to claim a kiss.

She gasped and dropped the bowls onto the dirt-packed floor in her haste to push against his shoulders. "Nay, sir. I'm not—"

Strong hands set her back on her feet, then shoved her would-be attacker off the bench to sprawl on the ground.

Her father's friend, the blacksmith, had arrived in time to defend her.

Again. 'Twas one of several reasons she preferred the kitchens.

Beacon's voice boomed through the now-silent room. "None touches the innkeeper's daughter without answering to the rest o' us."

"Begone. Ye're nay welcome here." Graham stood from the table and pointed a finger at the door.

The red-faced youth scrambled to his feet as if itching for a fight and scanned his surroundings. He swallowed hard before turning his attention from his glaring audience to her.

Wide eyes and a whitening face gave hard evidence that he'd not seen her scars before his attempted kiss. He stammered a quick apology and ran toward the door.

Proof yet again that no man would ever find her truly attractive.

With heat flooding her face, she ducked behind her curtain of hair and bent to retrieve the fallen dishes.

If she could only disappear to the kitchens and stay there.

"Our apologies, Maggie lass." The cooper cleared his throat. "We dinna ken the lad would try such a thing." He darted a quick glance Graham's direction.

Rising from her crouched position, she nodded at the cooper and faced Beacon. "Thank ye for yer help."

"Nay trouble." He cleared his throat. "Actually, I'm a hoping ye'll take it in payment for more of yer cooling salve."

She raised her eyebrow at the burly man. "Burn yerself again, did ye?"

Laughter rippled around them as she eyed the blistered skin on the forearm he thrust in front of her eyes. Black cinders speckled the surface of the wound but were hardly noticeable beside the rest of his soot-covered arm.

"Ye'll be washing yerself thoroughly first. I won't be a wastin' my supplies on ye otherwise."

"Aye, Maggie." His grumble brought a smile to her face.

"I'll be just a minute." She retreated to the kitchen with the dishes and returned moments later with the ingredients for the herbal remedy to find Beacon waiting at an empty table, his clean damp arms resting atop the wooden slats.

As she examined the edges of his burn, the other guests returned to their lively, gossip-filled discussion about the tanner's trip while Graham took over the ale and food service. Apparently, the tanner had also seen a Sutherland messenger near the Gunn keep, but the majority of the villagers were glad Isla had picked the Sinclairs for an alliance over their dishonorable neighbors to the south.

Moira ground comfrey leaves and lavender into a fine powder, then mixed them with honey to form a paste. Meanwhile, the tanner reported that the Sinclair laird and his son were coming soon to finalize the alliance and many agreed they would be glad to have the issue settled.

Although a few sitting in the room fondly recalled the days of Laird Angus before he married Isla, who'd brought her young son Roan with her from the MacDonald clan even farther to the south. Others recounted the events a few years later when Angus was bedridden with a mysterious illness and his daughter disappeared into the woods, never to be found. Her heirloom brooch on a bloodied cord was the only sign of trouble.

The lack of a thorough search, however, had made it clear that the captain of the guard—and Isla—believed her to be dead and her remains devoured by beasts.

Moira's heart clenched at the memories. She dared not look at Graham, who ducked into the kitchens, likely to check on the progress of yesterday's ale barrels since most of the guests sat dining on their stew and meat pies while swapping tales.

Apparently she was the only one reluctant to hear their clan legends, for even the traveling friar in the corner leaned forward to hear the chatter.

She spread the sticky salve across the blacksmith's burn as the villagers recounted how Laird Angus died from a broken heart shortly thereafter, leaving Isla to pressure the council to acknowledge Roan as his heir and then assume leadership on behalf of her minor son. Until the fifteen-year-old boy had fallen from a horse and died three months ago, leaving the entire clan vulnerable to attack and eager to forge alliances to ensure their survival.

Ignoring the speculation behind her, Moira cleared her throat and addressed her patient. "Now remember, you need to clean the wound twice a day and apply new salve."

Instructions she'd uttered so many times before for similar burns.

Beacon merely grunted in return.

As Moira reached for a rolled strip of cloth, the cooper's voice rose above the din. "If only Laird Angus's daughter were still alive. She'd be eighteen by now and allowed to rule."

Another scoffed. "As if we want another woman to lead us."

"But anyone would be better than Isla." A few of the men spat onto the floor in disgust.

With shaking hands Moira wrapped the bandage over the salve-coated burn and tied the ends together. Thankfully, only her foster parents knew her true identity.

Because she wasn't a leader.

And if Isla knew she was still alive, she'd send her guards to finish the task attempted so many years before.

With a quick reminder for the blacksmith to keep the fabric as dry as possible, Moira stood and gathered her supplies intending to retreat to the kitchen. And regather her composure.

Across the room, the door burst open, letting in a burst of sunshine, fresh air...and the Matheson girls.

Cara Matheson glanced around the room, tears streaming down her face. "Isla's soldiers are around the bend. Da is trying to stall them, but—"

"Please don't let them take us." Kyla clutched her sister's arm, the stark fear on her face underscored by the grim expressions of those who had already filled the room with dire rumors.

No one had been there in the woods to protect Moira five years before, but someone must do something to keep the girls out of Isla's jealous clutches.

And while she couldn't defend her clan, she could help these two.

With a flash of rage stiffening her spine, Moira left her herbs on the table and headed for Cara and Kyla. "Carry on as usual, men. I'm the only girl ye've seen this day."

A few nodded, then the cooper launched into a familiar story while others forced laughter to fill the room.

Moira grasped the girls' hands and pulled them toward the empty storage bench in the corner where the friar sat. Young that he be, surely he would protect them with his silence, if not his robes.

* * *

So much for remaining inconspicuous on the outskirts of the talkative group.

Evan pushed aside his half-empty bowl of stew and rubbed a sweaty hand on the rough brown fabric of his borrowed robes as the serving wench drew closer with the frightened girls. What did she expect him to do? Pray for them? Hide them? Surely she knew that even a true man of the cloth couldn't offer sanctuary outside the walls of a monastery.

He drew a deep breath for courage. The next moments would likely expose him as an imposter.

A spy in their midst.

"Please rise, sir."

Momentarily stunned by her request, Evan blinked up at the dark-haired lass, then slowly stood. She grabbed his arm and pushed him aside before lifting the wooden lid of the boxlike bench he'd been seated upon.

As she helped the girls into the empty depths and instructed them to lie down, Evan scrambled to make sense of it all. The space had apparently been built for extra storage. Or perhaps to hide other contraband? Perhaps the integrity of the innkeeper who had disappeared into the kitchens a few minutes prior and those who worked for him wasn't to be trusted.

Yet despite being inclined to believe that the shocking stories he'd overheard about Lady Isla's rule were exaggerated tales, the villagers would not go to this extreme to shield two girls unless they truly feared for their safety.

Meaning 'twas the lady and her soldiers who were not to be trusted.

But he'd been raised with the expectation that a clan's needs always came before that of the chief, so to question the integrity of another leader without evidence seemed unjust.

What, then, was the right conclusion?

While a growing fire in his belly burned to discover the truth, he took care to keep an expression of calm indifference on his face and instead pulled on the constricting fabric around his neck.

The serving wench—Maggie, the men had called her—propped a few thin scraps of wood along the top edge of the box. Her focus remained on the girls lying below them, although her eyes darted every which way. "No matter what happens out here, you have to remain absolutely quiet." Her words could also have been meant for him.

The sisters nodded in unison, then disappeared from view as Maggie shut the lid, small gaps from the pieces of wood allowing for air flow, and motioned for him to retake his seat.

Thereby involving him in her scheme to hide the girls beneath his cleric's robes. Likely hoping they implied his innocence.

As he settled into place, he glanced up to find Maggie holding a finger to her lips. Asking outright for his silence and cooperation.

If only she knew the truth.

He couldn't cause a scene even if he wanted to, otherwise his own deception would be revealed to all.

Evan finally made eye contact with the lass, surprised by the mixture of fear and fierce determination in their violet-blue depths. She was a woman of striking beauty, one unlike any Maggie he'd known before. But up close, he also had an unobstructed view of the horrific scar that ran from the hairline above her right ear down beside her mouth, then to her neck where a thinner line marred her flesh.

Used to seeing his battle-scarred clansmen, it was as easy to recognize the clean slice of a dagger as the evidence of an inexperienced healer. How could such an injury have happened, and what pain had she endured during her recovery?

Curiosity warred with the reminder of the two girls hiding beneath him. He pulled his gaze from her injury back to her eyes. Despite the flash of pain in their depths as she'd endured his scrutiny, she yet waited for his agreement.

His nod sealed his fate.

She bobbed her head once in response, then turned to fetch another pitcher of ale. After refilling their cups, she spoke with a few of the villagers as if this were a typical noon meal. Only a slight crack in her voice signaled her distress.

Less than a minute later, Evan heard the sound of galloping horses outside. Moments passed before the door burst open and two dark-haired men with red shirts beneath their Gunn plaids shoved inside, filling the door with their broad shoulders.

The tables of saffron-shirted village men fell silent and stared. Based on a few nervous glances and his memories of the earlier conversations, the distinctively-clad newcomers must be the wicked Isla's henchmen. Obviously they'd been hired for their brawn. And the weapons strapped to their backs made it clear that resistance was futile.

Maggie stepped forward to greet them but kept her head bowed like expected of a humble serving girl in the presence of her betters. "If'n ye're looking for a meal, we've got fresh meat pasties and a hearty stew. Ye—"

"Nay." One of the men scanned the room, pointing his slightly crooked nose into everyone's business. Then ignoring the room full of men, he turned his attention to Maggie. "We're here about two lassies last seen running this direction."

His friend grinned, exposing a missing tooth. "We're to escort them to the castle so they can prepare for the marriage selection."

While Evan sensed the undercurrent of tension in the room, Maggie merely shrugged. "Could they have run home to gather their belongings?"

Evan bit back a smile at her words. It wasn't technically a lie.

She stepped closer and lifted her head to face them. "Should I pack a bag too? Maybe a Sinclair would pick me as a bride."

Her words and appearance shocked the soldiers into surprised silence. Their roving eyes stopped searching the room and focused on Maggie. 'Twas a brave act on her part, but Evan spotted her trembling hands clasped at her waist.

Crooked Nose waved a hand at Maggie's face and looked at his companion as another red-shirted man entered behind them. "Don't bother with this one. She's useless."

The toothless one nudged his friend in the ribs. "I can think of a use fer the hag...if'n I close my eyes."

Evan's stomach churned at their cruel words and his hands began to curl into fists beneath the tabletop. He should step forward to do something, just like before when the other man had pulled her onto his lap.

And yet, here he sat. Useless.

"What are ye' two blatherin' about?" The third soldier pushed around his companions, then blanched when his eyes settled on Maggie's face.

The lass appeared equally shocked to see the newcomer but lifted her chin and glared at all three men. "I thought all the maidens were being invited. Or is it only the pretty ones who get the honor?"

The third man looked at his friends, his frown accentuating the small scar above his left eyebrow. "Ye're right. This one's not wanted at the castle."

Maggie turned away from the soldiers and lowered her head again but not before Evan caught the flash of fear in her eyes. While he could understand bruised feelings over their insults, she should be relieved to be spared a trip to Isla's keep. So why the sense of panic as she retreated beyond the tables of villagers?

'Twas a riddle for a different time as the unwelcome visitors discussed their mission. After all, orders were orders and they could not return empty-handed. Crooked Nose offered to search under the tables in the inn in case the *hideous* serving wench was lying about seeing the girls while the lecherous Toothless headed for the adjacent kitchen.

At least Scarface went back outside to search the perimeter and watch the other exits.

Meanwhile, Evan vowed to never forget the trio's faces or their callous treatment of their own clan. He might not be able to do something today without revealing his identity, but once the rest of the Sinclairs arrived next week, he could see that justice was done.

As the other men in the room grumbled about being made to leave their chairs so Crooked Nose could peer underneath their tables, a slight rustle beneath him reached his ears. With a tap of his foot against the boards, he reminded the girls to remain silent in their hiding place.

By helping to shield the vulnerable, mayhap he wasn't useless after all.

Now was his chance to make a difference.

CHAPTER THREE

With Isla's guards distracted by their fruitless search under the tables, Moira cleared empty dishes to occupy her shaking hands and gather her wits. However, the longer the soldiers stayed, the more likely it became that they'd find the missing girls, and the village would pay the price for defying Isla.

But that was the least of her worries She closed her eyes and recalled the wicked gleam in Devlin's eyes as he'd met hers a few minutes earlier. After five years, her refuge had been exposed with a simple flash of recognition. It was only a matter of time before Isla's wrath focused on her again.

With a stack of dirty bowls in her arms, Moira turned toward the kitchen to find Graham grumbling from the doorway with his wife behind him.

"Me barley malt will overcook and be a wasted if'n they don't let me stir it." Lavena propped her hands on her hips. "Whoever they be seeking, 'tis obvious none be daft enough to hide behind the pots or in the blazing oven. Not when the back door already be open to let in a welcome breeze."

At least the couple could honestly pretend ignorance about the missing girls since neither had seen the sisters enter the inn.

"Hush. It'll only be a moment till he agrees with ye and leaves ye to yer spoon again." Moira set the dirty bowls in the tub inside the doorway to the kitchen, then held her arms wide so the brute stomping around the room and riffling through the cupboards—as if a body might fit in the cramped shelves—could see she had nothing to hide.

The man grunted and brushed past her to join his friend in the main room. "Nobody's in the kitchen. Any luck out here?"

"Nay. But I've got one more table in the corner to check."

Moira stared as the soldier swaggered toward the young friar and his treasure-laden bench.

While Graham and Lavena retreated with relieved expressions to their ale-making activities inside the small kitchen, she couldn't relax until the soldiers left the inn.

Someone had to protect the innocent.

And then she'd plan her own escape.

"Hey, good man." The visiting friar's cheery voice boomed across the room. "Did I hear ye say ye've come from the keep?"

"Aye." The soldier pulled aside a chair and bent to peer under the table.

"Ah. I'm a'headed there meself. Told to be there before Midsummer's Eve for the Feast of St. John the Baptist. Tell me, will there be a tasty feast?" The friar patted his stomach as if only concerned about his next meal. His half-reclined figure spread further across his bench as if he'd been there awhile and had no intention of moving anytime soon.

"Only the best foods for Lady Isla." The soldier waved a hand at the friar's stew bowl. "Much better than this slop."

The friar nodded, then sat up and reached for his cup. "Mayhap. But the ale makes up fer it. Must ye continue about yer business or could ye sit and swap tales fer awhile?"

She held her breath. Surely he wasn't asking Isla's guard to linger mere feet from his prey. And yet, the bold invitation clearly implied he had nothing to hide.

Along with the friendly expression on his face and the widespread Highlander belief that a man of the cloth would never lie.

The guard chuckled. "Alas. I canna. But if ye've been here awhile, ye'd surely recall if ye saw a pair of maidens."

The friar shook his head. "I've seen plenty of maidens in my travels, but I can honestly say I havena seen any run through here today."

"'Tis unfortunate, else my duties 'twould be done and I could sample the barrels."

Devlin chose that moment to return. "Any luck?"

His companions crossed the room to join him. "They aren't here." With a grumble, the trio left but not before Devlin glared in her direction as if to promise he'd be back to deal with her later when there wasn't an audience.

Moira's knees shook and she steadied herself on the closest table. His wasn't an idle threat, and the fiend would enjoy correcting his earlier mistake of letting her live.

The room waited in a silent hush until she heard the clipping of hoof beats outside. The blacksmith peered out the door to confirm the soldiers had indeed galloped away. At his nod, the villagers broke out in nervous chatter as they recounted their close call.

Moira stared across the room, the gaze of the young friar capturing her attention despite the noises and movement surrounding her. A shiver of awareness ran down her spine at the warm brown depths that matched his nut-brown hair, and she couldn't help but recall the scent of the outdoors that lingered on his robe when she'd pushed around him to hide the girls.

Shaking free from her foolish attraction to a friar, she whispered her thanks that he'd kept his silence about the hiding place. He nodded in return.

She'd caught him staring at her scar earlier, but now he looked her in the eyes as an equal. Even the other men in the room couldn't keep eye contact after all the years she'd spent among them, as if all they could see was her wound and not her worth.

The friar was different. Like God looked through his eyes to truly see her. Or mayhap he'd figured out her secret— that she pretended to be something other than what she was.

The cooper's boisterous voice intruded into her thoughts with a mimicking of the friar's words. "I can honestly say I havena seen any maidens run through here today." He chuckled. "Never known a church man to lie before."

The man in question broke their connection and turned toward the others with a shake of his head. "It wasn't a lie. I did not see them run through here." He stood and shook out his robes. "They may have run through the doorway, but once inside, 'twas a fast walk at best. And they did not pass *through*...since they are still here."

With that, he opened the lid with a flourish and reached down to assist the shaking girls from their cramped hiding place.

The villagers cheered, then raised their cups in a round of toasts to outwitting the dim-witted.

As the tearful girls emerged, clinging to each other in fear, the harsh reality intruded. Cara and Kyla might have escaped for the moment, but they could not return home else they be taken later. The guards might even have ventured on to search their family's home or used their temporary escape to teach a lesson to the rest of the clan.

The verra fact that the soldiers had come this far from the keep to round up girls meant there wasn't a safe place left in the Gunn holding to hide.

For them.

Or for her.

Devlin's initial shock had been replaced with a vicious resolve. Whether he returned today or reported back to Isla first, her time here was done.

She had to run. Now.

Moira stepped back into the doorway to the kitchen. "M...Ma? Da?"

Graham turned from the stove with a frown, then as if her face revealed all, dropped his spoon and hurried to her side. "What's happened?"

"'Twas him. He was here searching for the Matheson sisters. Out there." She fingered her scar. "He knows I yet live."

Graham's eyes widened in shock, flitted over her shoulder to the celebration in the main room, then shifted back to her with flames of righteous indignation in their depths. As if he would fight to protect her.

But he was too old to fight.

Yet when Devlin returned—as he was sure to do—he would question the villagers as to her identity. And the dear couple who had helped her heal, called her by a new name, and started their lives over on the outskirts of the Gunn holdings just to protect her would suffer his ire.

She'd brought danger to their doorstep. How could she repay their hospitality by making them a target of retribution?

Moira clutched his arm and eyed a shaking Lavena. "People here know ye claim me as daughter, so when he returns, ye canna pretend I'm a stranger to ye. Ye'll have to hide too."

"Nay. Yer mother be too auld to start over again." Graham cut off his wife's protestations with a shake of his balding head. "There be fewer questions if we stay. Besides, I can honestly say I found ye in the woods near to death and delirious with loss of blood. Mayhap ye didn't ken yer own name, so how would I?"

Moira glanced again at the woman who had sat by her bed for days. A blanket of grief draped over her shoulders at the sorrow shadowing their eyes.

They knew the somber truth even if her stubborn heart refused to believe it.

This was goodbye. Perhaps forever.

She'd known the day would eventually come as they aged, but to have it thrust upon her so suddenly under the threat of violence? 'Twas too soon, and yet she wasn't a child anymore.

Unlike the girls she'd hidden away less than an hour ago.

She glanced over her shoulder to see the friar a few feet away, nudging the girls along before him.

Somehow she'd find a way to survive, at least until the Sinclair alliance was forged and she knew if they would bring peace to the lands. Or strife if they were worse than Isla in demeaning the common folk. Mayhap they would simply allow Isla to continue reigning as an honorary leader.

If so, Moira might never be safe again. But in the meantime, she could make her life count for something, starting with protecting the Matheson sisters.

She sidestepped to allow the girls entrance into the kitchen. "I'll take Cara and Kyla with me into the woods."

"The nooning crowd be leaving soon. If anyone asks after ye, I'll tell them ye're searching for more herbs for yer mother."

She nodded. "Where should we hide?"

* * *

Evan stopped in the doorway leading to the sweltering kitchen. Should he reveal that he'd overheard?

His eyes darted between Maggie and the old couple with tears in their eyes. A mixture of fear and inexplicable grief hung thick in the room. What was it the man said about not knowing her name?

Evan cleared his throat. "If I may, ye probably know the woods around here better than I, but in my travels I happened upon a dry cave about a half day's walk northeast from here. It would provide adequate shelter and protection for a short time."

As the trio swiveled to face him, the hairs on the back of his neck also rose, alerting him to the quieting of voices in the main room behind him. The villagers had picked up on the tension. While he hoped none of them would betray their own, especially after maintaining their silence mere minutes ago, one couldn't accidentally—or under torture—reveal information they didn't have.

Evan nudged Maggie, her parents, and the two recently-hidden sisters further into the kitchen and shut the door behind him.

"Northeast a half day's walk, ye say?" The older man stroked his chin.

"Aye."

Maggie's eyes widened. "That's almost to Sinclair land. Would we truly be safer there? I thought to head west to—"

"Nay." The old man shook his head so quickly that his graying beard swung across the front of his saffron-dyed shirt. "The outcasts dwell there. And Isla's guards wouldna expect you to go toward the Sinclair border. Even without reinforcements it could spark a war instead of an alliance if her warriors ventured that close."

A shiver ran up Evan's spine. His clansmen would never believe that armed soldiers searched for mere girls…assuming they asked questions first before eliminating a perceived threat.

"But the Sinclairs? We donna ken if they be fair minded, especially if they're forging an alliance with Isla. Will they take advantage—"

"Hush, child." The man rested gnarled hands on Maggie's slim shoulders, then pulled her into an embrace. "Donna frighten the others with wild talk. God still reigns over both our clans."

Evan bit his tongue. Their uninformed indictment stung, but he didna dare reveal his identity by defending his family.

However, the sooner the Gunn people could meet the Sinclairs, the better. As long as his father didn't seem to approve of Isla's actions and the behavior of her thugs.

Yet another reason to return home with the information he'd gained in his short travels on Gunn land. Would the council believe him without proof? Would they laugh at his tales? Or simply ignore him like usual?

He had to try. But after doing a small part to conceal the sisters mere minutes ago, he also desired to see them—and now Maggie—to safety.

The older woman led the girls over to a cluttered table and began a whispered conversation. Evan doubted she knew what really brought the sisters to the inn. It had all happened so quickly that those in the kitchen must not have realized the truth of why the soldiers had come.

After all, Maggie had been the one to decide to hide them, not her parents. His eyes drifted back to her pale face. He couldn't shake the overwhelming desire to learn more about her and the mysterious story that brought her to this place. In this condition. And what caused the fear currently shaking her body?

Could he offer protection and also deliver the news? He needed to travel that direction either way, and delaying the family reunion for another day or two would not change the outcome much.

And yet... He pushed aside his questions and looked toward the innkeeper. "Sir? Ye donna have much time."

Tears ran down the old man's face as he released his daughter.

Maggie stared at the older man as if she was afraid she'd never see him again. The innkeeper might not be her real father, but her loyalty was evident. Along with her hesitation to leave him behind and venture alone into a harsh world.

Suddenly, Evan's decision was made. At least he could be a hero to her—and the other girls, Cara and Kyla—before returning home.

He cleared his throat. "If it pleases ye, I can escort them to the cave and stay long enough to see them settled."

"'Twill ease my mind and that of me wife." The older man nodded, then gave the now-gasping Maggie a gentle shake. "Ye need to hurry, lass. Run home with yer mother and pack a bag of extra clothing to share with the other lasses. They canna return home for their things."

Maggie swallowed hard. "I'll need to take my medicinal herbs."

"And yer dagger. Gather a couple blankets and another bag o' foodstuffs. Donna linger."

She nodded, then dashed through the back door with the older woman trailing behind her.

The man turned to Evan and pointed toward the closed door to the main room. "I'm Graham, by the way. Can ye tell them we're closing early today? Collect their coin and dishes?"

"Aye." Anything to ease the man's burden since his daughter—and valuable helper—was leaving so suddenly. As Evan opened the door, he overheard Graham issuing more orders for Cara and Kyla to wash the dishes and help him pull the last meat pies from the oven. 'Twould do them good to keep their hands busy. And their minds distracted from the reality that they were also leaving their families behind with no opportunity to say goodbye.

Evan clasped his hands at the waist of his borrowed robe and raised his voice to those seated in the main room. "Graham said to tell ye he's closing early today. I'm to collect yer coin and dishes."

Several men simply nodded and rose from their seats to file toward the door. Others lingered with questions.

"The lasses will be taken care of and the less ye know, the better." Evan stared down the most inquisitive of the bunch until they nodded.

The boisterous storyteller from before clamped a hand on Evan's shoulder. "Tell them I'll be joinin' ye in prayers for their safety."

The larger man with the freshly-bandaged arm tugged his friend toward the door. "And Friar, we all pray for deliverance from those who would keep our people captive to fear."

Evan swallowed his guilt over his continued facade and nodded. Though a pit settled into his stomach at the thought of staying quiet, 'twould not be wise to reveal his identity now…especially when he couldn't guarantee his father would bring justice.

With the last of the villagers gone, Evan latched the front door, then cleared the tables before returning to the kitchen. Lukewarm wash water splashed over his forearms when he dropped an armload of dishes into the tub in the kitchen. He grabbed a towel and rubbed the rough fabric against his skin before joining Graham at the high worktable.

In exchange for the fistful of coins collected for the earlier meals, he was given a bulky bag and a litany of instructions.

"I've a feeling she's leaving us for good." The wrinkles on Graham's face had settled into a grim expression. "Taught her to use these years ago knowing that someday she may need them to survive. Never thought the day would come without warning."

Evan peeked inside the bag, and his eyes widened at the bow, arrows, and snares. Could the man truly have believed danger was inevitable enough to warrant keeping such things at the inn?

Graham cleared the emotion from his throat. "Now, ye'll need to stay off the road…" The man continued with a description of a few of the landmarks Evan had passed a few days before.

'Twas tolerable to endure the man's rambling lecture knowing that it stemmed from a father's love. Yet as he was ordered to take care of Maggie at all costs, Evan's shoulders sagged under the weight of responsibility for another's welfare.

The sacred role of protector was being passed to him.

If only Graham knew Evan's true identity.

Then again, God did. And it seemed that, like Esther in the Scriptures, mayhap he'd been placed here—in a rundown inn on the outskirts of Gunn land—for such a time as this.

"She'll worry herself about us, but I've lived off the land myself before and can again if needed."

Having assumed the role of temporary guide, Evan found himself getting antsy. 'Twas not time to linger. They needed to get away from the inn before the soldiers returned. Especially since the brutes were on horseback and their haphazard traveling party would likely only have one palfrey amongst them, if that. After all, his riding horse would be more of a handicap to their visibility than a help to ease their load. Not to mention that with his supposed vow of poverty, he would only draw more questions and attention. He would have to carry his own burdens.

At the reminder, Evan slipped away to the main room and retrieved the pack containing his belongings, including his small sword.

Back in the kitchen, he found that Maggie had returned, a lumpy pack strapped to her back and tear-stains on her face. With a firm jaw, she called for the girls to dry their hands and pick up the additional bags of food and water skins her father handed them.

Meanwhile, he pulled a few coins from the pouch hanging at his belt and another half-truth from his mind. "I've been tasked with the delivery of a palfrey and left it at the stable." His own beast. To be delivered back home, preferably with him astride. "Will ye see to boarding the horse while I'm gone? I'll return later to retrieve it or send someone in my stead." He passed the coins into Graham's shaking hand. "By the way, my name is Evan."

Graham tightened his fingers around the coins. "A strong name. Means God is gracious."

"He is." A sense of holy warmth drifted around his heart. Mayhap God's grace was being extended through him. 'Twas a thought to ponder later once they were away.

The group huddled near the back door while Graham scouted the cleared area between the inn and the nearby woods. He returned a moment later with a nod. "Brother Evan, will ye beseech Heaven on our behalf?"

Of course the man would ask. After all, Evan was supposed to be a man of the cloth.

Evan closed his eyes and dug deeply into his childhood memories of Father Tomas praying before the family. His heart beat fast with the potential falsehood he was about to speak, but he led the group in a short—but honest—prayer before adding a personal silent petition.

God, please keep us safe.

CHAPTER FOUR

Moira wiped perspiration from her brow and released a deep breath as a breeze rustled through the trees. Two hours after they'd left the inn, the cruel hand of panic clutching her gut had finally eased. If her group were being followed, they surely would have been discovered by now.

After leaving the inn, their foursome had cut through the woods and crossed the creek upstream of the bridge rather than risk being seen on the open road. A friar and three lasses traveling together were sure to attract attention from even the least curious among their neighbors, let alone the ordinary travelers passing through.

With Friar Evan leading the way, their single-file procession meandered through the wilds hemmed in between a rocky stream somewhere on their left and through the trees to their right, the dirt road leading to the Sinclair holding.

'Twas slower to pick their way over the rocks and around the brambles but safer nonetheless.

By unspoken agreement she brought up the rear of their group behind the Matheson sisters. Neither of them spoke a word, but the occasional sniffle broke the silence.

First from fear of discovery. Or perhaps shock at being so suddenly uprooted from home.

But now? Perhaps the others were lost in thought or, like her, worried about the future. Or simply weary from their obstacle-strewn flight.

Moira stumbled over a branch hidden beneath a pile of leaves and staggered to catch her balance. While used to being on her feet all day, this longer trek while carrying a loaded pack had drained her strength.

If it were truly a half day's walk to the cave, they still had a long distance to travel before evening fell. They'd need to keep their energy high to make this journey successful, but had no time to linger for a meal—or chance to risk the Gunn soldiers finding them upon their trek. The hairs on the back of her neck prickled against the unknown. After pulling a fistful of dried beef and loaf of bread from her pack, she hurried to catch up with the sisters.

"Cara, 'tis a wee bit to tide ye over till evening. To give ye strength as we walk." Moira tore off a chunk of bread for the lass then another for Kyla, who had stopped on the path ahead.

"Thank ye." Cara's hesitant smile spoke more of her gratitude than her words as she accepted the offering.

With a quick nod, Moira moved on to feed the other sister. "Ye're doing well to keep up our pace."

A handful of steps later she'd caught up with their broad-shouldered guide. "Friar Evan, is it?"

"Just Evan will do."

She frowned. Mayhap the familiar address 'twas part of his penance, but the man still needed to eat, so she held out the meager snack. "I ken 'tisn't much, but since we canna stop..." Her words trailed off at the surprise in his warm brown eyes.

Was he unused to gifts of kindness? Or mayhap he thought her offering an insult? As if he were as weak as a lass? Or did he think that being a friar meant he must ask or beg for every meal? 'Twas no time for that here.

Her errant thoughts stalled at his quick nod.

"Thank ye." A slight smile curved his lips as he reached to take the food. His fingers brushed the palm of her hand, and a tingle ran up her arm to settle around her heart.

She remained rooted in place as the friar—Evan—continued forward to blaze their trail. The sisters also passed by. Moira fell in behind them and had consumed half of her meal before she fully acknowledged the sense of connection that bound her to the friar.

Something similar had happened during his prayer before they left the village, and she couldn't discard or explain the feeling she'd met him before.

Or maybe 'twas simply because he served the Almighty God and she herself used to easily pray.

Before.

A renewed stirring within brought a whispered prayer to the surface. A silent plea for safe travels and protection from those who sought them harm.

Along with a deep longing for justice, even though she'd never voice those dormant hopes.

She brushed the last bread crumbs from her hands and took a drink from the water skin hanging around her waist before truly absorbing her surroundings for the first time in hours.

Without the fear-induced blood pulsing in her ears, she caught the familiar woodland sounds of her childhood. The trickle of water in the distance and the slight crunch of pine needles underfoot. The chirping of birds and the rustle of leaves overhead as a slight breeze cooled her face.

With the distant rugged peaks and dense trees along the riverbeds, her clan's homeland was a beautiful place. Too bad she might at this very moment be leaving it behind in her quest for refuge.

Could she really leave her kinsmen?

An uneasy sensation swirled within her along with the unwelcome thought that perhaps she should stay to defend her home.

As if a mere lass could resolve what her father's soldiers had been unable to prevent.

Steps ahead of her, Cara and Kyla now talked quietly between themselves, wondering aloud if their father had been beaten for causing the soldiers' delay or if he too had been warned to go into hiding. Of course, that scenario assumed that Graham had been able to send the family a message about their daughters.

Her heart pounded when Kyla glanced back at her with a frown crossing her fair face.

What if Graham got caught delivering such a message? Or Devlin returned demanding answers about her whereabouts? Retaliation from the frustrated guardsmen would be likely.

Would the villagers also be caught in the fray?

And what about Sheena? The lass was on her way to the keep now and walking directly into the path of danger.

If any of the rumors were true, Heaven help her and the other girls already there.

As if aware of the rising agitation behind him, Evan glanced over his shoulder at them. "Since ye're now in the mood to talk, I could tell ye the tale of the frustrated fox."

"A fox?" Cara glanced around the woods.

"Aye. 'Twas not too far from here." The friar chuckled. "I spied a fox chasing a rabbit until it disappeared down a hole beneath a log. While the hungry fox dug and scratched to widen the opening, behind a rock not six feet away a half score of rabbits exited a different hole and made their escape."

Evan embellished the tale with what he imagined the rabbits saying to their forest friends the next day, and Kyla giggled.

When it came to distractions, there was wisdom in his storytelling, even if he hadn't done it on purpose. 'Twas better to keep one's mind busy than centered on things one couldn't control.

While the girls recounted tales of their own to entertain the friar and each other, Moira put the same lesson into practice by collecting additional herbs and sections of bark to supplement her stock of remedies. Only Heaven knew what she might need in the coming days. Between her brief forays off the path, she eyed the man leading them. 'Twas odd to see a man hampered by a brown-woolen robe striding through the woods as confidently as her father's plaid-clad warriors strode across the training grounds.

Perhaps 'twas because his age seemed more near her own than any other priest or churchman she'd ever met, but she wondered how he'd come to serve the Church instead of choosing another vocation.

Like her, he seemed more comfortable out here in the woods than in the group of strangers back at the Inn.

The sun sank low in the western sky when Evan angled farther from the road and toward the creek. He pushed ahead to break a path through a wall of brush. "Isn't far now."

Eager to reach their destination and set up camp while they still had light, Moira caught up with the sisters and urged them forward as she passed them by.

A crashing ahead on her left was followed a moment later by a large animal bursting through the trees. The wild boar came to stop on the path a stone's throw ahead of her, its chest heaving with exertion.

Despite Kyla and Cara's high-pitched screams behind her, Moira's feet stayed rooted in place as the waist-high beast turned, then eyed her with a malevolent gleam. Blood pounded beneath her cheeks, the scar on her face burning with the remembered pain of the knife slice from five years ago. The boar's razor-sharp tusks could easily inflict the same agony.

Ahead of her, a war cry echoed through the woods. Evan had dropped his pack and was in the process of drawing a sword from within its depths while using his voice to attract the danger toward himself.

When his second yell diverted the beast's attention, she turned to lead their escape, only to find the sisters already halfway up the closest tree. But while they were high enough to find safety for themselves, there wasna room for Moira to also perch on the fragile limbs.

Instead she dashed past them to a different refuge, dropped her pack beside the trunk, and reached for a low-hanging branch to pull herself up.

At a squeal behind her, she glanced over her shoulder.

Too late to escape.

The beast had charged.

And too-far behind it ran the warrior-like sword-wielding friar.

* * *

Beyond the charging boar, Maggie's face drained of color. Her grip loosened on the branch as her expression shifted from stark fear to a hint of something else.

Almost a resignation as if she knew her time had come.

Not on his watch.

Digging deep to the untapped warrior within, Evan roared loud enough that her eyes widened in surprise. The beast slowed and began to turn, hesitating enough for Evan to close the gap between them and ram his sword through the animal's neck, nearly severing its head from its body. but not before a tusk sliced a white-hot gash along his forearm.

Heart pumping, Evan swung the sword a second time to pierce the animal's chest and confirm its death. Standing over the boar brought a unique thrill of victory. No wonder his brother and the rest of his father's warriors loved their training so much. If he'd been half-hearted before, he now determined to hone his skill even further.

While he dinna wish to raid or wage war like some of his clansmen, protecting the innocent was a righteous mission.

Chest heaving from his effort, he lifted his gaze from the motionless carcass to find Maggie staring with a mixture of awe and gratitude in her eyes.

Tears filled those eyes before she turned to help the other two lasses down from the branches. Once on the ground again, the trio clung to each other. Why did women feel the need to cry so much? Must be their way to shed the excess emotion.

The same emotion he felt fading from his own frame, leaving behind a mixture of euphoria and weariness. And the sharp awareness of pain radiating from the injury on his arm.

Turning from the sight of the women consoling each other, he used the bristly hide of the boar to clean his sword before retrieving his pack and stowing the weapon back into its depths. He used the small dagger at his belt to cut a strip of cloth from the hem of his robe and wrapped it around his wound to staunch the flow of blood.

'Twould have to do for now.

He shouldered his pack and rejoined the women in the middle of the slight clearing, just steps away from the beast that could have...

"Almighty God, thank ye for yer hand of protection this day." The whispered prayer of thanksgiving burst unbidden from his lips.

The sisters whispered their amens whilst Maggie gazed at him with something akin to adoration blended with disbelief. Her lips moved silently as if adding to his prayer.

His eyes swept over the area. What other dangers lurked in the bushes? While their screams might have frightened off additional beasts...they could have simultaneously drawn the attention of any human searchers.

They needed to be on their way again. And soon.

"The cave is close. Let's get moving so we can get settled afore dark."

While the lasses scrambled to gather their dropped belongings, he knelt to hack a chunk of meat from the side of the boar. There wasn't time to butcher it all, but they'd have fresh meat tonight.

Along with a new tale to tell.

Maggie held out a cloth to wrap the meat. "At least something good came of this encounter."

He returned her smile while she stowed the bundle in her pack, then nodded before leading she and the Matheson sisters toward their destination. The close escape added extra energy to their steps, but he still took care to choose a path that would leave little trace of their passing. As the sun slipped behind the distant mountain peaks, they reached the hideaway he'd discovered on his way to the Gunn holding.

A place God Himself must have known these girls would need later.

He held back the bushes shielding the entrance of the cave and motioned the others inside. "Head back around the corner. There's a wider spot with a natural chimney to let out the smoke while not allowing the light to be easily seen from a distance."

"Did ye stay here afore then?" Maggie stopped beside him while the other two ventured farther inside.

"Aye. Left a small stack of wood too. Enough to start a fire for light and get the meat to roastin'."

Dim twilight filtering down from a distant hole in the ceiling cast thick shadows as he knelt beside the ashy remnants of his former fire. He cut shavings from a fresh stick of wood, pulled a piece of flint from the pouch on his belt, and struck it against his dagger blade. Almost afore the girls had sliced the meat into thin strips that would cook quickly, a crackling fire lit the rocky chamber.

He stood and replaced his tools at his belt. "If ye hand me yer water skins, I'll see to refilling them, then gather more wood."

Maggie shook her head. "The light be fading fast and two be getting the task done in nay time."

"Verra well." He handed the older sister a handful of twigs that would work as skewers for the meat, then followed

Maggie out of the cave. Once past the row of bushes, he led her along a faint animal trail to the nearby stream. "Donna be long."

While she refilled their water supply, he kept an eye on her and quickly scavenged around the base of the nearby trees until he had an armload of wood. By the time he was ready to return to the cave, she was on his heels, two sloshing skins dangling over each shoulder.

The lass surely wasna afraid of hard work. And dinna easily fall to complaining, which couldn't be said about the lasses he'd grown up around.

With darkness upon them, he was pleased to see no sign of smoke coming from the cave. Or light.

In fact, if it wasn't for the aroma of roasting meat wafting from the entrance, he'd have walked past their hideaway.

Once he and Maggie made their way back inside and the lasses had taken turns seeing to their personal needs outside, he joined the others in tearing pieces of somewhat-charred meat from the skewered sticks and washing it down with fresh water. His hunger finally sated, Evan noticed that the lasses had organized their supplies along one wall and laid out blankets nearby.

As tempting as the warmth might be, he wouldna be sleeping near the fire tonight. He was there to protect their lives and it wouldna do to destroy their reputations in the process.

Better not to sleep at all.

He added another log to the fire, then extended his hands toward the flames to soak up as much heat as he could while it lasted.

Maggie gasped. "Ye're wounded."

"Aye." He glanced at the now-crusted bandage. With the sleeve of his robe inched higher, the blood-soaked fabric looked more-than-gruesome in the firelight. With the visual reminder, his sluggish brain acknowledged the dull throbbing that he had ignored for the past hour.

"Let me see to it."

Mayhap her herbal treatments would be wise, but the mere thought of her hands on his skin sped up his pulse. A supposed friar would never have such thoughts.

"Nay." His voice came out harsher than he'd intended, and he softened his tone. "I'll see to it while I'm standing watch this night. Ye need to rest whilst ye can."

"If yer sure." She frowned, her pink lips pursing slightly as if debating how to make him submit to her ministrations.

Lips that an ordinary man would be tempted to kiss.

But he was no ordinary man, especially while masquerading in his borrowed garb.

Robbed of words, he simply nodded. She shrugged her slim shoulders, then curled up in a blanket and lay down near the other girls. The dimming firelight reflected off the unscarred side of her face as she stared into the flames.

He turned away lest she catch him staring.

As much as he dreaded the thought of soaking the bandage off in the cold stream and trying to clean the wound himself, mayhap the pain would keep his mind off foolish thoughts about the lovely maiden whose life he'd saved.

He rose to his feet and headed toward the entrance to the cave, almost tripping over the confining fabric of his robe in his haste.

'Twould be a long night.

CHAPTER FIVE

Moira awakened to a deep-seated chill and a dull ache in her hip and back. Almost as if she'd slept on a bed of rocks.

She blinked and observed her surroundings. Oh, wait. She had.

Yesterday's events came crashing back to the forefront of her mind. It had taken a long time to fall asleep beside the now-cold fire, then in her dreams she'd been chased by visions of a wild boar with Devlin's face and haunted by memories of the feverish pain that followed.

She thought she'd outgrown the nightmares years ago, but now they'd returned with a fresh twist, leaving her somewhat groggy and with a lingering sense of disquiet.

The best cure had always been to focus on the day ahead rather than the pain of yestereve.

After stretching the stiff muscles acquired from hours of hiking through the woods, she sat up and looked around their temporary home. The girls were still asleep, tear-stains resting on Kyla's face, but Evan was nowhere to be found.

She'd have thought him gone except that his pack leaned against the stone wall, the blanket she'd left for him still neatly folded beside it.

She ventured outside to see to her personal needs, then made her way toward the creek to wash her face and work the tangles from her hair. Once she was presentable again, she'd have to start on breakfast. Perhaps she could make a porridge of sorts in the small pot Graham had added to her pack. If he'd taken the time to include cooking supplies, he must believe she would be without a proper home for a long time.

Lost in thought, she didn't notice Evan crouched beside the creek until she was almost upon him.

"Good morn." He waited for her reply with a weary smile upon his face.

"And to ye." She eyed the dark circles underneath his eyes and the pallor of his skin. Appeared he hadna slept at all while watching over their safety.

"'Twas seeing to a bit of breakfast." He pointed his dagger at a string of fish anchored in the flowing water, then returned to cleaning and filleting the trout in his hands.

She knelt upstream of his fish-gutting task and dipped her hands into the icy water. Splashing it upon her face brought a quick gasp from her lips.

And a chuckle from her nearby companion. "'Twill wake ye for sure."

"Aye." She smiled and quickly finished the task, drying her chilled hands on the plaid still draping her plain gown. Moving to sit on a nearby log, she ran her fingers through her thick hair until it lay somewhat smooth over her shoulders and to the middle of her back.

Tempted to plait it out of her way like she normally would when working at home in the kitchens, she instead once again left it loose as a curtain. She'd caught the curious stares of the Matheson sisters and didn't wish to make them uncomfortable. 'Twas hard enough for them to be separated from home without being forced to spend time with the village oddity.

Evan cleared his throat, and she glanced over to see him staring in her direction. Had her scars caught his attention? Or her hair?

Unexpected heat rose in her face.

He held up the fish neatly skewered on green sticks that were less likely to catch fire. "I hate to intrude while the others be abed, but didna ken if ye could start these a'roasting by yerself."

"Aye." She stood and took the fish. "If'n a spark be needed, I've a flint o' me own in me pack."

"Good." His smile widened. "Keep it small and I'll watch for smoke while I refill our water."

She nodded and hurried back to the cave. After leaning the skewers against a stone, she moved the water skins to the cave entrance, then returned to blow the embers of the previous fire to life before adding a bit more fuel.

Last night's greasy meat had cooked in its own juices but the fish might be dry. She hated to ruin Evan's work, but perhaps a few herbs as seasoning would help.

She dug through her supplies and soon sat upon the cushion of her folded blanket, twirling portions of fish over the crackling fire. The aroma woke Kyla and Cara, and soon their foursome was gathered around the cheery fire, each roasting their own breakfast.

Kyla giggled. "Never thought I'd spend a night in a cave and cook fish over a fire."

Cara frowned. "'Tis better than being halfway to the Gunn keep this morn."

Her sister shuddered. "If rumors be true, 'twould be worse than getting gored by the boar yestereve."

Moira rotated her stick of fish to apply heat to the other side with a fresh awareness that she was blessed to be alive. Like her whispered prayer after their near escape, she should have spent more time over the years being thankful...and less time questioning God's will for leaving her with a scar. Mayhap spending time with the friar had turned her mind toward a proper view of the Almighty.

Kyla's groan interrupted her musings. "Wish my ma had taught me the proper way to cook a fish. Mine's going to be half raw and half burnt."

Evan pulled his meal from the flames and poked a finger at the seared flesh. "Mayhap we'll get better with practice."

Moira bit her lip. "Or mayhap next time I can use the pan I found in the bottom of my pack. Had wondered if I carried rocks."

"Now she tells us." Evan growled low in his throat.

She glanced at him through her curtain of hair. "Ye'd already skewered the fillets afore I had a chance. Didna wish to injure yer feelings."

He mumbled something about women which caused the Matheson sisters to burst into laughter. Moira threw back her head and joined them.

A moment later, Evan also chuckled, then grinned at her, a twinkle in his brown eyes. "Ye should look up more often."

Her smile faded. What did he mean?

Memories of the past few years paraded across her mind. She'd been looking down and away from people for years trying to hide her identity…and her scar.

But Evan had seen her flaw and still smiled at her. And so had Cara and Kyla.

The pleasure of their acceptance faded as quickly as it had come. Mayhap she didn't need to hide her scar, but even her friends couldn't handle the burden of her identity.

What if someone else recognized her?

She ate the rest of her meal in silence as the others talked among themselves in quiet voices. Once done with her fish, she tossed her stick into the flames and stood, eager to be alone with her thoughts.

She'd always done her best thinking whilst moving.

"Now that we've got light, I'm going to get the lay of the land and see what other herbs I can find." She slung her medicine bag over her shoulder and headed for the entrance.

"Donna go far." Evan's deep voice held a thread of concern.

Feeling protected rather than stifled, she nodded, then stepped outside. This time she turned away from the water and circled the rock formation enclosing their cave. The fresh air did wonders for her spirits and she soaked up their peaceful surroundings. Like in other parts of her homeland, dense stands of trees were interspersed with thickets and flower-dotted glades heralding the warmer days of June.

Could she really look up more often?

She raised her eyes to the heavens, her hair falling free behind her.

Before her an outcropping of comfrey lay among the pile of rocks. 'Twas timely since she'd used most of her supply for Beacon's salve just yesterday.

With a laugh at God's timing, she scrambled to collect an abundant supply of the precious herbs. 'Twas exactly what she might need to treat the angry gash on Evan's arm if he didna let her see to it soon. He might be stubborn about accepting help, but she'd find a way to do so later.

Her smile faded. Growing attached to the friar wasna a good idea. Like others in his order, he'd made a vow never to marry. And even if he could, he was too good for her.

Not to mention, his good looks and easy smile attracted attention. How could she even consider an attachment to the friar when she needed to stay hidden to stay alive?

Jumping down from the rocky perch, she spotted a fallen tree. The kind of spot bees often picked to build their hives. With the cool air of the morning keeping the bees docile, she managed to avoid getting stung while filling a small leather pouch with sweet honey, then added it to her medicinal supplies. To think that such a treasure lay hidden behind the branches of a dead tree. Just like their cave lay behind…

Nay, that single row of bushes didn't offer much of an obstacle in the daylight. Mayhap if she added more branches it would look more like a bramble afore a rock wall.

Or she could weave a leafy tapestry to cover the opening.

* * *

Maggie should be back by now.

Evan leaned against the cave wall near the entrance. The shocked look in her eyes after his teasing comment worried him.

Had he upset her unduly when he told her she should look up more often?

After watching over her during her restless sleep—disturbed by obvious nightmares—he was even more emotionally invested in her wellbeing than he should be.

What did she fear?

And why did he care?

Was it her rare beauty? Her work ethic? The compassionate way she looked after the others that attracted him the most?

Or was he merely fascinated by the possibility of a mystery to unravel?

He fingered the wet edges of the bandage on his arm, as annoyed with his fixation on the innkeeper's ward as the condition of his wound. Last night's haphazard cleaning in the dim moonlight hadn't been ideal, and this morning, after soaking the old bandage off, he'd wrapped the oozing wound in a fresh—albeit slightly unclean—strip from the hem of his robe. The accidental soaking while fishing for their breakfast likely hadn't helped either.

What was it Maggie had told the blacksmith yesterday? To keep his burn dry? Was it the same for other wounds?

He shrugged. He'd ask her later if she ever returned.

In the meantime, he'd attempt to gather more information from the chattering sisters who were busy sorting their food supply and wondering if they could bake some sort of bread atop the stones. 'Twas as if they'd already forgotten yesterday's scares and found comfort—or distractions—in the familiar tasks.

He bit back a smile as one even mentioned making some sort of a broom to sweep the cave floor. As if they would be staying in the cave indefinitely rather the fortnight remaining before the alliance was forged at the altar.

Assuming his report home did not halt the proceedings.

"How long have ye lived in yer village?" He glanced back over his shoulder, addressing the question to the elder sister.

One question led to another until he had a somewhat clear picture of village life. Cara shared that Maggie's family had only lived in the area for a few years but that the Mathesons didna know where they'd been afore that. That at eighteen, Maggie didna spend much time with the younger folk.

Kyla mentioned that she and Cara personally were fifteen and sixteen and both vying for the attention of a handsome lad who seemed more interested in the miller's daughter who used to work at the inn afore she set her sights higher and headed off to at least get hired at the keep.

Their answers painted the picture of childish lasses who had been pampered and sheltered by their family—as lasses should be. Not immature, but until yesterday's scare, they'd been innocent of the pain the world could bring.

Unlike the wide range of emotion he'd already seen in the depths of Maggie's eyes.

Maggie.

Should he go looking for her?

He shifted to begin walking out of the cave in pursuit of her but stopped his movements when he spotted her approaching from further downstream with an armload of branches.

"Thought 'twould be good to add more camouflage around the cave entrance." She nodded to the animal trail leading to the water. "And we'd do well to scatter needles along this path and vary our own excursions otherwise it points right to us."

Her concerns set his legs to moving once more and hurried out to take her burden. A sharp twinge in his arm warned that he ought to take care lest he start bleeding again.

"Ye're a smart lass." He caught the blush coloring her cheeks and couldn't resist teasing her further. "Are ye sure ye aren't a military commander seeing to the defense of our wee castle?"

She sucked in a quick breath and snapped her gaze to his. Captured for a moment by the swirl of emotion in her eyes, he reluctantly broke the connection and turned toward the cave with the load of branches.

For a moment he harbored a foolish thought at the sparks between them. But nay. He could not provide for a wife...yet.

If there were to be a marriage alliance forged between their clans—without Isla at the helm—the bride would be for his older brother, not he.

Disappointment clawed at his stomach and weakened his knees.

At least the first bride was spoken for. But mayhap he would be allowed to further the alliance later with another match.

Distracting himself from the errant thoughts, he focused instead on the task at hand to make the cave a safe hideout for more than just a night. As Maggie set the younger girls to weaving a tapestry of vines and leaves to hang over—and shield—the cave entrance, he wedged the branches into place, then ventured out to gather more from assorted places.

Hours later, and despite a quick nibble of cheese drawn from their supplies, his legs weakened. Likely from a lack of sleep, but he could only rest once he knew Maggie, Cara, and Kyla were safe. He wouldn't fail them.

With wood, flint, blankets, water, and now adequate camouflage, all the lasses needed was a supply of food to supplement the dwindling perishables they had brought with them.

And since he would soon leave to rejoin his family, he needed to confirm what the innkeeper had said about Maggie knowing how to catch fish and set snares.

While she scattered pine needles and created a decoy path away from the cave, he ducked inside to retrieve the bag Graham had tasked him with, stopping beside the chattering sisters putting the finishing touches on their weaving just inside the entrance. "We aren't out of danger yet. Voices carry in the woods and we aren't as far from the road as ye may think. If someone was to come a'searching today…"

Cara stopped midsentence and Kyla's eyes widened. They nodded, then lowered their voices to a mere whisper.

Leaving them to complete their task, he soon reached Maggie, who was surveying their handiwork, and held up the snares. "Do ya want to come along to set a few? See about some supper?"

Her eyes lit up as if with a somewhat happy memory and she nodded. "If'n we get more meat than we need tonight, we should smoke some for later."

He nodded, then led the way further upstream as he eyed the underbrush.

"There?" Maggie's whisper captured his attention as surely as her light touch on his elbow did. She pointed to a break near the base of a tree.

His smile grew. 'Twas the perfect place for a rabbit den.

Indeed, Graham had taught her well.

His joy at discovering her resourcefulness in the woods warred with fresh disappointment. Perhaps she didn't need him as much as he longed to be needed.

They worked together to set the snare and camouflage it with more leaves. In the process, her silken hair fell like a russet curtain between them. Like before, his fingers itched to brush it away from her face. Instead, he distracted himself with finishing the task and moving on to find a second location.

As he scouted the area, his heart beat with uncertainty. She might not need his help with the snares, but he could still take advantage of their time together. Perhaps this was the ideal time to learn more about her and the trouble haunting her dreams. Especially since her personal fears seemed to have begun when facing off with one particular soldier at the inn.

He kept his voice low. "If I may say so, it seemed one of the soldiers yesterday recognized you."

"He…he should. He's the one that did this to me, and as the captain of her guard, 'twas most likely under Isla's orders. Probably thought I was dead."

"How long ago?" He forced the words out of a throat choked with burning rage. Isla and the guard must pay for hurting an innocent lass.

"'Tis been five years now."

"When ye were scarcely a child?"

She released a bitter laugh, her fingers reaching for her neck, then falling away to scatter more leaves. "I'd reached a half score and three that verra day."

"What happened?" And more importantly, why?

"Devlin found me in the woods outside the keep." She paused as if reliving the moment that likely fed her nightmares, leaving a heavy silence between them. "Tried to slit my throat, but when my knees buckled, he lost his grip and the dagger slipped up my face instead."

He couldn't fathom her fear at having a dirk at her throat.

She shook her head as if ridding herself of the memory. "In the confusion, I was able to get away and eventually I stumbled upon Graham. He took me home, and his wife cared for me."

"What about your family? Don't they know you're alive?"

"Mother died when I was verra young and my da died soon after this." Her finger ran along the scar on her cheek. "I had no one to go back to, just the couple that took me in."

The couple that called her Maggie even though Graham mentioned not knowing her name.

Violet blue eyes stared deep into his soul. "That's why I'm so afraid that Devlin will tell Isla I'm still alive and report where he saw me."

"Why did she want you dead in the first place?"

His question hung in the air between them as they set up a second snare, then moved further along the edge of stream. Would she honestly answer his question? Or did she even know the truth?

When she finally spoke again, her voice held the weight of years of pain. "Jealousy of me mother perhaps. Or mayhap she wanted me to marry her son when I was older, but I wasn't good enough. She always picked at my flaws and banished me from many a meal as punishment."

He knew what 'twas like to always bear the criticism of others.

But could Isla truly be driven to jealousy by a commoner? And yet... "Do ye think she's truly hurting the girls who come to stay at the keep to prepare for the alliance?"

Something niggled at the edge of his mind. A marriage alliance hadn't been necessary or even considered until a few months ago, so why injure Maggie five years before?

"She is." The pain in her soft whisper broke his heart. "And 'tis my fault. I was the first, and mayhap if I'd returned to confront her, she wouldn't feel free to hurt the others. Although I can't show up now. If I do, I'm as good as dead."

"Donna worry yerself. I'll protect ye." He made the hasty vow, then recognized an inner sense of resolve as if he'd found his true calling.

And yet his talk today had only brought her pain to the surface.

He strode to a log and patted the bark beside him, determined to bring a smile to her face. "If ye grew up around the keep, there must have been a happy time that ye remember."

CHAPTER SIX

A happy time?

Moira sidestepped a patch of wildflowers as she approached Evan's perch.

Would it be too revealing to say 'twas now? To be walking in the woods with a man who saw past her scar?

To have his questions turn from the harsh retelling of the day that forever changed her life?

To savor her relief at not needing to continually guard her words so as not to accidentally reveal her identity?

She sat beside Evan on the rough log, then sighed.

Isla had more reason than jealousy to see her dead, especially now that her son was no longer alive to inherit the lairdship.

Moira shook off the morbid thoughts and tried to recall the days before Isla.

The days when her mother was still alive. Her smile grew.

"There it is. I knew there had to be a good memory somewhere."

She caught her breath at the carefree grin on his handsome face so close to hers. It wasn't right to notice a friar as if he were an ordinary man.

CANDEE FICK

"There were happy days." She closed her eyes and lifted her face to absorb the dwindling warmth of the sun on her skin afore the gathering clouds blocked its heat.

He nudged her shoulder with his. "Like when?"

"Like when we gathered in the Great Hall for a feast. I still can recall climbing onto my mother's lap and hearing the music. The laughter. And even the soldiers telling their stories…stories my mother thought were too gruesome for young ears." Was that too revealing? While she'd eaten all her meals with similar experiences, even the crofter's children had enjoyed the festivals when the clan gathered as one.

He chuckled. "All mothers must feel the same across the Highlands, for mine also scolded the warriors."

Good. He hadn't found her memories unusual.

But thoughts of her mother brought back even more recollections. Like the hours spent beside the fire stitching a tapestry portrait of their family to hang alongside those of other Gunn lairds before them.

Or the day her parents entrusted her with her mother's wedding brooch, which had been passed down from the generation before. The same heirloom she later wore on a leather cord.

She fingered the light scar on her neck. The same one Devlin had ripped away before he'd tried to kill her.

"You know, I visited the Gunn keep before, when I was a young lad during a visit with my mother." His tone softened. "Back at the inn, I heard the stories about Angus and his missing daughter."

A shadow fell across her happy memories and a chill skittered across her skin.

"I actually remember the little tyke. She followed me around everywhere I went."

Moira stilled her hands in her lap and feigned interest as he told a tale of exploring the grounds while the men had talked of political changes on the horizon.

Yet inside, a storm of emotion swirled.

While she dinna remember him, would he eventually recall her? After all, she still remembered the servants whispering about her distinctive eyes. Another reason to keep looking down.

On the heels of those thoughts came another regret. Only the members of important families ever visited the keep. If his mother had been a guest, he was far above her current station even if he had pledged himself to the church.

As his story wound down she diverted the subject from her clan's lost princess. "How did ye come to know so much about survival in the woods?"

He grimaced. "Actually, my tendency to wander off backfired on me once, and I vowed I'd never be so afraid again."

"What happened?"

"Oh, I was about a half score and three when my father took my brother and me along on a clan hunting trip. In the excitement of killing and the resulting butchery to harvest the meat, I got distracted exploring a nearby animal's den. And then I was left behind."

He frowned. "No one noticed my riderless horse, presumably because they'd loaded the carcasses upon it. I spent a long two days wandering through the woods in the general direction I thought I needed to go before being found by an old woodsman. He took me home where I soon discovered that no one had even noticed my absence."

Her heart ached at the confusion in his voice. How could a family not notice their missing child?

He cleared his throat. "I decided then and there to learn as much as I could about survival in the wild so that the next time they left me behind, I'd have more to eat than a handful of berries."

No wonder he'd grown up and decided to join the church so he could be somebody important. Somebody who would make a difference.

She reached out to comfort him, but he flinched when she touched his bandaged arm.

"Oh, I can make ye a—"

Afore she could mention a salve for his wound, he clamped a hard hand over her mouth with a whispered, "Whist," in her ear.

Her impulse to struggle against his strong hold died at the realization he stared back in the direction of the cave.

She held her breath and listened for whatever had caught his attention. There. The snort of a horse and the creaking of leather.

And the deeper sound of men's voices carrying on the wind.

Before she could gather her wits, Evan pulled her to standing and tugged her deeper into the nearby thicket.

After a quick glance at their options, he stopped at the base of a large leafy tree and pointed up, then cupped his hands as if to give her a boost.

With renewed panic flooding her veins, she sped upward through the branches with Evan on her heels, hoping the inevitable rustling of leaves was masked by the nearing sound of angry voices.

Halfway up the tree and high above the ground, Evan settled onto a sturdy limb facing away from the water and pulled her onto his lap.

She pressed her lips together to silence her squeak as he anchored her in place with a strong arm around her waist.

A moment later, the argument halted just a stone's throw away.

"I thought I heard voices hereabouts. The brush is too thick back there, so they must have come this way."

She turned her head to stare into Evan's wide eyes, then glanced down to catch a glimpse of red through the leaves.

Isla's soldiers stomped along the creek bed where the horses they led had room to maneuver.

And somehow, her plan to add more branches to their hideout—in the verra direction the men had come from—had somehow blinded them from discovering the Matheson sisters.

One soldier kicked at the log where she and Evan had sat moments before. "Blast the captain and his demands that we bring that scarred hag in for questioning."

The captain? Devlin?

'Twas clear they were searching for her since she was the only one with scars.

She shuddered, then burrowed closer to Evan's chest as if she could disappear into his protection. His arms tightened around her, echoing his earlier promise to keep her safe.

But as the warmth of his body seeped into the icy dread chilling her bones, she became aware of his firm thighs beneath her. And the disturbing realization that in their scramble upward through the branches, the fabric of his robe had bunched beneath her, giving her a glimpse of his bared leg when she glanced toward the ground again.

On the heels of that inappropriate observation came another chilling pronouncement from the searchers. "We must be getting closer to the cave."

"He said it's along the creek but not too far from the road."

Others knew about their cave.

And someone had told Isla's henchmen that Moira was heading this way.

A shiver ran up her spine at the implication that one of her clansmen had betrayed her.

* * *

Evan tightened his hold on Maggie and pulled her trembling body closer against his chest.

If only he had his sword—but he'd left it behind with his pack in the cave. With only a mere dagger at his waist, their silence 'twas their only defense against the search party beneath their feet.

That and Heaven above to watch over them.

"We must have come too far along the road on horseback." He recognized the nasally tones of the one he'd dubbed Crooked Nose.

"Aye." Ah. Toothless had joined his friend. "We should have forced our informant to come with us."

Maggie stiffened in his arms, but despite her silence and only knowing her for a day, the same piercing betrayal coursing through her also ran through him. Someone in the village had revealed their destination.

Yet, as the soldiers meandered further from the cave...and back in the general direction of the village, perhaps the person had only done so under duress.

One could hope.

While the sounds of their pursuers gradually faded into the distance, his mind drifted back to the revelation that their captain—the scarred one Maggie had called Devlin—sought the woman in his arms, not the girls that had evaded them yesterday. Paired with what he now knew of Maggie's story, there could only be one reason.

To finish the job and silence her forever.

He couldn't fight the soldiers on his own. 'Twas urgent he return to his family to rally their support, but he must see Maggie to safety first. While the clear road home beckoned, he could not risk leaving them so exposed.

After waiting another minute to confirm the soldiers were not returning, he relaxed his grip on her waist. "We must be away."

She nodded, then took a deep breath before easing away from him.

Their stealthy journey out of the tree taxed both his patience and his injured arm as he lowered her one limb at a time. With frequent pauses to make sure their noise had not caught unwelcome attention, they reached the ground without trouble.

The sun had disappeared behind a large cluster of darkening clouds while they had been shielded within the tree, and the rising wind blew Maggie's hair around her face.

As if they needed another obstacle to overcome. But while a storm would slow their escape, enough rain could also hinder their pursuers.

While he retrieved their empty snares and used a branch to erase all signs of their being in the area, Maggie took a moment to twist her swirling hair into a knot at the nape of her neck, clearly revealing her pretty face…and the stark scar, a cruel reminder that the danger to her life yet lingered.

Within a few minutes of hurried yet cautious walking, they arrived back at the cave to find the sisters had already put out the fire and begun packing their belongings.

Tears streamed down Cara's pale face as she whispered, "I've never been so frightened in all my life."

"Especially since…since we didna ken where ye were." Kyla's voice wobbled.

Maggie rushed to give both girls quick hugs before rolling their blankets. "Thanks to Evan's keen ears, we were hidden up a tree whilst they walked right beneath us."

He brushed past them to place the snares into their bag. "'Twas too close of a call and we can't risk their return." He hoisted his pack onto his back, wincing at the renewed throbbing in his arm. A glance at Maggie caught her frowning at his bloodied bandage.

"I should—"

He cut her off with a shake of his head. "There's nay time now. We must—"

"Find a new hiding place and put more distance behind us." She glanced at the others and sighed. "As much as I hate to leave our cozy nest with a storm brewing, safety comes first."

Once again feeling the weight of their trust upon his shoulders, Evan led the group across the water and deeper into the woods, heading downstream from where the soldiers searched and angling somewhat closer to Sinclair land in the process.

The steeper terrain on this side of the river made for slower progress. Rain that began not long after they left the cave soaked through their clothing, but none of the girls complained. Mayhap the reality of escaping twice in a matter of two days motivated them to keep walking hour after hour. Yet, the farther they were from the road, the safer they'd be.

As the light began to fade on another day, Evan stumbled upon a clearing sided by a large formation of rocks.

Aha. A familiar landmark.

If his memories of the map on his father's wall were correct, they were not far from the border with Sinclair land. Another creek a stone's throw beyond the clearing should lead to a valley that cut into the heart of the Gunn holding...and the keep where Isla reigned.

For now, however, the overhanging rock wall would provide a bit of shelter from the wind-driven rains. 'Twas unfortunate everything was so wet because a fire would have been welcome.

As his companions huddled together for warmth next to the rocks, Evan searched for a few sturdy branches, then drove them into the soggy ground to support a sodden blanket over their heads. As shelters went, 'twas sadly lacking but 'twould have to do until morning. But with a nearby water source, the clearing would make a good location for their new camp once he was able to build a proper shelter with the rocks to protect their backs.

Once he had done all he could for the time being, Evan wrapped himself in another wool blanket, and with an empty stomach and shivers cramping his spine, he settled in for another sleepless night a respectable distance away from the others.

CHAPTER SEVEN

Moira had never been so happy to see the dawn.

After a long cold night spent huddled beneath a dripping wool canopy, her muscles had settled into a perpetual cramp, and the gnawing sensation in her middle reached through to her backbone.

Yesterday's fish on a stick and the small chunk of cheese at noon were a distant memory. And after their exhausting trek through the heart of the storm, a meal had been the last thing on her mind.

However, despite the lingering misty drizzle, the rising light brought hope that today could be better than the days before, and as she spied Evan reclined against the rock wall a stone's throw away, she abandoned her former complaints. After all, their protector had spent the night exposed to the elements.

Moira worked the kinks out of her stiff fingers, then dug around in her pack for the last of the dried beef. 'Twould have to do until they could hunt later. Or even build a fire to cook a pot of porridge using the sack of meal Graham had put in her pack.

After handing a few pieces of meat to Cara and Kyla, she eased out of their shelter and crossed to where Evan guarded their glade.

"'Tisn't much but 'twill have to do." She held out the larger piece of the remaining meat.

He accepted her offering with a weak smile, then tilted his head in invitation for her to join him.

Leaning against the rock wall beside him, she forced herself to chew her portion slowly and savor the moment of refreshment.

A minute later, he broke the silence. "This clearing will be a good place to make camp while ye wait for the search to end."

Her stomach cramped at the reminder that there were those who wanted her dead and her companions carted off to the keep against their wishes. They'd need to remain in hiding at least until Midsummer's Eve.

"I'll stay long enough to build a proper shelter for ye and the fire. There's another creek not far." Evan pointed across the clearing to a break in the trees.

She studied their surroundings as relief washed over her. Situated far from the main roads and likely near the Sinclair border, chances were slim anyone would stumble upon them here. 'Twas the ideal place to settle for some time.

But 'twould take a day's worth of work from all of them.

Moira swallowed the last bite of her beef. "After all the rain we've endured, I canna believe I'm a'saying this, but I'll refill our waterskins."

Evan offered a weak smile. "I can start with the support beams, but mayhap the lasses will weave us another tapestry or two of branches for a roof and walls."

"We can gather firewood too." Cara's voice alerted Moira to the presence of the other two girls.

Kyla groaned. "Not that much'll be dry."

"Yet." Evan pushed aside his rain-soaked blanket and dug around in his pack before pulling out a small ax. "I've a feeling the sun will yet shine today, and in the meantime, our activity will help to warm us."

After draping the worst of their wet things over a few nearby bushes to start drying, Evan headed into the woods with his ax, and Moira led the others in the direction of the creek.

Once she'd taken care of her personal needs in the privacy of a nearby thicket, she knelt beside the trickling water and scrubbed the muddy grime from her arms before lifting handfuls of fresh water to her face. 'Twasn't the same as a warm bath with a change of dry clothes, but ridding herself of the grit seemed a momentous accomplishment sure to improve her outlook this day.

Upstream, the younger lasses giggled and gasped as they did the same.

If only Moira could wash her hair, but perhaps plaiting it would keep it from accumulating more dirt and leaves. And since the girls now appeared comfortable around her scars, perhaps they wouldna mind her practicality.

As she worked the worst of the tangles from her hair with her fingers, she caught the distinctive sounds of an ax chopping into wood far behind her. Evan must already be making progress on their shelter.

She divided her hair into thirds and began to weave the sections while planning how to organize their camp. Closer by, feminine voices carried on the breeze and interrupted her thoughts. She turned to scold the Matheson sister about being quiet, only to find the girls staring at her with wide eyes.

The silent girls.

The trio scattered behind the closest bushes an instant before a small group of women reached the creek from the opposite side.

Clad in the familiar Gunn plaids over their plain gowns, the others appeared to be in their late teens. And all seemed wet and miserable like they too had spent the night hiding in the woods.

With not a man in sight.

Cara and Kyla surged forward to greet the others, but Moira took a moment to loosen her hair down around her face. One never knew when she might be recognized. Staying behind the sisters, she peeked through her curtain of hair at the others. Then gasped.

One of the women had partially healed burns covering part of her face, neck, and down one arm. Another woman held a bandaged arm around her midsection and walked as if holding broken ribs while being supported by a younger girl.

Several conflicting thoughts hit Moira all at once.

If Isla was indeed the cause of the other women's injuries, then justice must be done. And soon. Meanwhile guilt cramped her stomach. Her people were suffering because of her silence.

And yet, fear intruded. She had to know the newcomers were alone before revealing herself and hearing their stories. Then they needed to get back to Evan so he could help her take care of them all. He'd know what to do.

Taking a deep breath, she moved past Cara and Kyla to address the newcomers. "Are ye alone? Who knows ye are here?"

After glancing at each other, the burned girl stepped forward. "Only our families know we are traveling this direction." Her gaze flickered to Moira's scar and she winced. "But I ken yer caution."

Moira nodded. "If ye have all yer things, follow me."

A few minutes later they stepped into the clearing. Beside the mountain of rock, Evan dropped his armload of longer logs and turned. His eyes widened as his gaze darted from one bedraggled girl to the next, lingering only for a moment on the injured few with a tight expression on his face.

She motioned the others forward. "Appears we're not the only ones sheltering in these woods. And instead of looking after two sisters, I've now seven to hide."

Her words seemed to shake the newcomers from their stupor. They surged forward to greet the friar as if the presence of a churchman gave them permission to confess their fears and thoughts all at once.

He raised his voice to be heard above the chatter. "One at a time, if ye please."

A pudgy redheaded lass took the lead. "I'm Birkita. Me sister and I are from Keirfield in the west and have been traveling this direction and sleeping in the woods for the past week." She glanced at the injured ones in their group. "We joined up with them two days ago. We're exhausted and the food our parents sent is about gone. My da said to seek refuge with the Sinclairs, but I fear we're a long way from there since we canna travel verra fast."

Evan nodded. "While the Sinclair border is near, 'twill take several days on foot to reach a village. If ye're healthy." He frowned before looking at the burned woman. "What's yer name and yer story?"

"Finella." With a halting voice, she told the story of going to the keep and being singled out for attention by the old laird's wife. True to the rumors spreading through the land, Isla had tripped her, and then sent her away without benefit of any medical treatment.

"The worst part of seeing her get hurt was the satisfied smile on Lady Isla's face as she turned away from the fire." The woman with the bandaged arm stepped forward and shuddered. "She just flicked a bit of ash from her sleeve and asked who wanted to take Finella's place of honor beside her. I refused and she went into a rage."

The two women shared a pain-filled look as stunned silence fell over the clearing.

One of the younger girls who bore a strong resemblance to Finella cleared her throat. "After Finella and Akira were brought home to Braighwick in the back of a hay wagon, our families feared the soldiers may return to silence them. Or take me in their place. That's when they decided to take action."

"Action? Ye mean send ye away?" Cara wrapped an arm around her own sister. Who knew what would have happened to them if not for Moira's quick actions?

"Yes. And nay." Finella shook her head. "Like Birkita's da, our families wanted us to find a safe place to hide and possibly get a message to the Sinclairs. But in the meantime, they are spreading the word and attempting to gather the clan afore Midsummer's Eve. If our new ally canna stop Isla's madness, the men intend to stage an uprising. She doesna deserve to speak for our clan anymore."

Grim expressions settled upon the faces of the group. A confrontation between Isla's trained men-at-arms and their ordinary kinsmen would prove deadly. And if Isla's spies heard the new rumors, she'd send her men immediately to eliminate any sign of revolt.

Starting with the living evidence of her insanity by chasing down these girls.

Would those guards find her too?

Nay. Evan promised to protect her.

And he'd protect the others too, wouldn't he?

* * *

Evan clenched his jaw as the two groups of women swapped stories about their travels and hardships along with hugs and more than a few tears.

The horrific rumors about Isla were true and the evidence stared him straight in the face. No doubt about it. His spying excursion was over. Time to get the information back to his father as soon as possible, especially since it seemed at least some of the Gunn men believed the Sinclairs were honorable and would come to their rescue.

Why else would they risk sending their daughters alone into the woods while they rallied their clan to fight? And yet, if their small group hadn't stumbled upon them, these newcomers would never have survived the journey without help.

There was safety in numbers...and a higher risk of discovery.

'Twas obvious the new women were in no condition to make another trek, but Maggie kept looking at him like he would be able to take care of them all. Like he was a hero.

He couldn't disappoint her, despite his own weariness.

"We're pleased to have ye join our wee camp and rest yerselves fer a few days." He raised his voice to be heard above their chatter. "But as ye can see, we've a fair amount of work to do. Once we've built a proper shelter, I'll need to leave to fetch help and more provisions." He eyed the cluster of seven women between him and Maggie. So many mouths to feed. "I can travel faster than all o' ye and besides, I know the way to the Sinclair keep."

Where he could accomplish two missions at once.

"However..." He frowned to silence the protests his words brought. "In the meantime, I urge ye to be as quiet as possible since high-pitched voices such as yers carry on the wind. *Ye* are fleeing a possibility. But, just yestereve, *we* had human searchers on our trail." He waved a hand in the opposite direction from the creek.

His words were met with wide-eyed shock, a hint of fear, and then a sober resolve.

Maggie pushed through the others to stand by his side. "Together we can be strong. After all, as my da used to say, 'Gunns never quit.' " She glanced up at him with a small smile. "Brother Evan here will do the heavy lifting, but each of us has something to contribute."

A chorus of murmurs and nods met her words.

After asking Finella and Akira to meet her by the rocks so she could tend to their wounds, Maggie sent the healthy girls into the woods to gather semidry firewood and materials to weave together into a roof and walls. Which was good because busy hands and minds had less time to worry. And less time for complaints about being wet and cold in the continuing drizzle.

Discouragement over the situation settled into his stomach, but he pushed aside the feeling and returned his attention to the shelter. Now that their group had expanded and required more space, he would need to make another trip to the woods for more logs.

If only wielding the ax didna make his injured arm ache so much.

He hoisted the ax over his other shoulder as he staggered back into shadowed forest, determined to do what he could for the women. With pain spreading higher up his arm, the wound 'twould need looking after soon, but could wait until the shelter was erect.

By the time he'd dragged a half score of freshly hewn posts into the clearing, the energy gained from the dried meat he'd eaten to break his fast had long since disappeared. Evan wiped the sweat from his forehead, then rested a shaking hand against the solid rock as he fought the dizziness threatening to overtake him.

"Here. Looks like ye need this." Maggie stood beside him with a filled waterskin.

"Thank ye." He guzzled the lukewarm liquid, then waited for his stomach to stop churning.

She waited for him to take another drink before returning the skin to their pile of belongings. "Can I help?"

He searched the pile of rocks for eye-level cracks where he could wedge in the roof supports. Finding several, he nodded. "I'll dig the holes, then ye can steady the posts while I pack the earth tight. After that we'll lash the posts together using the thinner poles and anchor them to the rock." Except instead of rope, he'd likely need to cut more strips of fabric from the hem of his shortening robe.

The temporary disguise he couldn't wait to be rid of.

One hole at a time, the framework slowly came together while nearby, the other women made progress weaving a large mesh of greenery for the roof.

Yet, the stronger the structure became, the weaker he felt.

After tripping over a rock on his way to grab the last horizontal branch, he paused with his hands on his knees to recover his balance, then slowly stood.

"They will not judge if ye need to rest." Maggie's murmur, despite calming his racing heart, did little to change his perception of his role within the group.

"Nay." He shook his head. "I'll rest when 'tis done and we're out of the rain." Not to mention, everyone else—including the injured girls—had followed Maggie's example and found a way to help.

Forcing himself to concentrate on something other than the pain throbbing across his forehead, he talked through their remaining tasks. "Once I secure this last post we can layer a few thinner branches across the top to support the roof. Perhaps the others can fetch a pile of leafy boughs to set beside the rocks to use as a mattress. 'Twill raise ye off the soggy ground until it can dry."

He wedged one end of the pole into the crack between the rocks, gripped a strip of cloth in his teeth, and raised the other end of the pole to meet the corner post that was already joined to the remainder of the front wall.

Maggie steadied the post as he quickly wrapped the binding in and out of the wooden supports.

"If we can get a fire started, I'll look to do a spot of hunting or fishing for food." Evan tied a knot in the fabric and pulled tight, giving the joint a small shake. 'Twas as solid a shelter as he could make with the materials at hand, and he couldn't have done it without Maggie's help.

A gust of wind blew a chunk of hair across her face, blocking her face from his view. Over the last few hours of work, she'd gone back to hiding her scar behind the curtain of hair. His fingers itched to push it away so that he could take in every inch of her.

Didn't she realize her value?

Would she believe him if he told her?

Perhaps 'twould be better to show Maggie how he felt.

Giving into temptation, he brushed the silken strands away from her face. "Maggie…"

Her vibrant eyes met his and his heart raced at the admiration shining in their depths.

"Ye're so lovely." His gaze dipped to her lips. Despite his attraction, 'twas too soon for kisses, and yet...

He lowered his head to brush a kiss across her soft cheek instead, but dizziness flooded over him and he grasped her waist to maintain his balance. His vision swam and he fought to remain upright, but his knees buckled and darkness descended.

CHAPTER EIGHT

Moira staggered as Evan's considerable weight threw her off balance. The physical contact was almost as surprising as the searing heat of his lips on her skin.

What kind of friar would kiss a girl, even if it was on her cheek? Hadn't he taken a vow of chastity? Then again, what sort of girl was she to seek out reasons to stay near the man? Hero-worship had taken her senses and invited his familiarity.

But no more. She pushed against his shoulders, and he crumpled into a cloth-covered heap at her feet before she could slow his fall.

Her initial shock at his behavior turned into panic when he didn't move. Just as she'd toed him with no resulting effect, sounds from around the clearing reached her ears.

"What's wrong with him?" Birkita dropped an armload of firewood beneath the rocky overhang. Hopefully she'd only seen him fall and not the actions that preceded it.

Moira quickly knelt to brush the hair from his flushed face and gasped. "He's burning with fever."

And besotted fool that she was, his illness had gone unnoticed or been explained away as ordinary exhaustion.

"Help me drag him closer to the wall." She grasped under his arms and pulled while two other girls rushed to help lift his limbs.

While a feverish delirium could explain the kiss—and his crazy mumbling about her beauty—what would cause such a strong man to drop into a faint?

'Twas almost as if he had an infection—

Heaven help her, she'd forgotten all about the wound on his arm from their encounter with the boar. She'd known it bothered him, but they hadn't the time for medicines while on the run.

And he'd worked so hard today. For all of them.

A minute later, with his body laid out along the back of their would-be shelter, she reached for the foul bandage and nearly gagged at the putrefying mess beneath the dirty cloth.

The oozing gash reaching from his wrist almost to his elbow hadn't been properly cleaned that first night and the wet bandages had allowed it to fester. And now, beneath the skin, dangerous red lines stretched toward his upper arm as the infection spread.

This wound needed to be cleaned and treated in all haste if Evan were to recover.

She reached for her satchel of herbal remedies and began barking orders for someone to fetch fresh water from the creek. With the rest of the women still occupied weaving the roof for the shelter, Moira sacrificed her spare gown to the blade of her dirk, creating a pile of clean bandages and a supply of rags for the task ahead.

The moment she touched a water-soaked cloth to his arm, Evan roused with a moan and a slap of his free hand as if to push her away.

"Nay. Like it or not, ye're staying put until I can clear the gore and pack yer wound with my herbs like I shoulda done two days ago."

He lay back with a sigh. "Do yer best, me bossy beauty."

Heat rose in her face at his delirious ramblings, but she focused instead on the task at hand. Once the wound was cleaned and snippets of rotting flesh removed, she mixed and applied a poultice to draw out any remaining pus.

The night of the boar attack she would have sewn the gaping flesh together, but now 'twould only trap the infection inside. Better to keep it clean and wrapped tight even if it left a thicker mark once it healed.

After a clean bandage was tied in place, she crushed a few other healing herbs into a cup of water and forced the mixture down his throat. Thanks to yesterday's exploration around their cave, she had a plentiful supply and didna need worry about running out.

All that remained was to bathe his fevered face with cool water and pray the illness hadna spread too far in his body.

Tempted to stay by his side, she instead eyed the unfinished shelter and dreary weather. If they didna wish to spend another sleepless night shivering in the rain, there was much still to be done.

After packing away the herbs and new bandage material, she reached for her comb and worked the worst of the tangles from her hair. Loose 'twould only continue to get in her way, and 'twas about time she stopped hiding the truth. Or at least part of it. Besides, if Finella could openly show her angry burns, how was a healed scar any different?

With quick fingers plaiting the strands into a rope-like braid, Moira called Akira over to Evan's side. "I ken ye canna do much because of yer arm, but can you keep bathing his face with the cold cloths? And offer him as many sips of water as he'll take."

The girl nodded, her eyes focused on Moira's exposed scar. "I'll be glad for something useful to do."

Moira smiled as she secured the end of her braid with a strip of leather, then dug through their belongings to find the snares. "And while ye be at it, mayhap ye can think of creative ways to cook a rabbit. Assuming I can catch a few and we can get a fire started somehow."

Behind her, another voice spoke up. "I ken how to fish."

She turned to find the other girls had gathered around. A few gaped at their first full view of her scar, but the moment

81

passed into a camaraderie born of necessity and shared hardship.

Soon they divided themselves into three groups for roof-raising, food-finding, and fire-starting. The girls scattered to their various tasks, for the sooner they were done, the sooner they could get out of the weather and enjoy something to eat.

Minutes later Moira tramped alone through the woods in search of a thicket with signs of a rabbit den. If she and the others were successful, there would be plenty of food soon and a dry place to rest. Perhaps with enough extra meat to smoke ahead, this camp could last until after Midsummer's Eve when they'd know if 'twas safe to return home.

Or they'd have provisions for a trek to seek refuge on Sinclair land instead.

By the time she'd returned from setting the snares, a watertight roof covered the top of the frame Evan had built, and several girls worked on a wind-breaking wall for one end. Near the wall but out of the rain, a mostly-smoking fire burned, and Cara stirred a handful of berries into a pot of porridge.

Moira's stomach growled in anticipation and she hurried to join the others awaiting a taste and warming their hands near the fire. After eating her share, she took a portion to Evan and Akira, then resumed her efforts toward a secure campsite.

Later in the evening, after a meal of fish, Moira took over the nursing duties for a still-feverish Evan while the rest of the weary travelers snuggled together under damp blankets on a bed of leafy boughs.

While 'twasn't a stone cottage or a solid castle wall, their shelter was sturdy enough. Based on their light snores, the day's work and a dry place to sleep made it easy for most of them to finally rest.

If only she could say the same for Evan.

The fever continued to plague his body, and he tossed and turned, stilling only when she placed another cool cloth on his forehead.

Or whispered a prayer in his ear.

Prayers for his survival and complete healing. After all, they needed him to go for help like he'd said.

But her guilty conscience wouldna let that reason stand alone. Even if it branded her the worst of sinners, she needed him to recover simply because she'd come to care too much for the handsome friar.

* * *

Dawn arrived with a touch of sun and more than a ray of hope. The soft chirping of birds replaced the patter of rain on the leaves and the bright green grass glistened with dew drops. From beneath a cluster of bushes, Moira watched a rabbit emerge with a twitching nose, then hop away in the direction of her snares.

She lifted her eyes heavenward in prayer. Heaven willing, mayhap they'd have more food for today.

After stretching the kinks out of her back, she left the shelter to see to her personal needs and check her snares. By the time she'd returned with a trio of rabbits dangling from her hand, the others had also awakened.

All except for Evan.

After his restless night, he slept soundly and his skin felt cooler to the touch. She changed his bandage and applied a fresh comfrey poultice to his arm, the wound a deep pink rather than a bright red.

Thank ye.

The girls broke their fast together with another pot of porridge, then scattered to various housekeeping and scavenging tasks as Moira prepared another remedy to help the other injured ones with their pain. She sent Akira out to sit in the sunshine and soak up the warmth before turning her attention to Finella.

"Do ye wish me to help ye apply more honey to yer burns?"

"Aye, but do ye also have any fresh bandages? The honey truly helps but it sticks to me clothes and pulls."

"Of course." Moira rummaged through her new supply and returned with a handful of bandages and her half-filled pouch of honey.

Tears leaked from the corners of Finella's eyes as they worked together to smooth the same type of salve she'd used for the blacksmith over the worst of the girl's charred skin and wrapped loose strips of cloth over the injuries hidden beneath her gown.

"The herbs will speed yer healing, but I've heard that honey alone will also help the scars to fade. We'll keep applying it several times a day until it runs out."

The girl nodded, then slipped out of the shelter to cry in private.

Moira weighed the rapidly emptying pouch in her hand, a sinking feeling dropping from her heart into her middle. She needed more honey if she were to continue helping Finella recover, but the downed tree from which she first gathered it was hours away and too close to danger along the road.

So much had changed in the past three days since she'd left the inn. Back then, her biggest concern had been her mother's aches.

And her visible flaws keeping her from ever finding a home of her own. She ran her fingers over the puckered flesh. If only...

"One scar does not define you."

Moira spun in the direction of the voice and found Evan watching her from his resting place. "Yer awake. How do you feel this morn?" She stepped quickly to his side, taking in his clear eyes, then touched his fever-free forehead. A tingle ran up her arm at the contact and she used the pouch of honey as an excuse to turn away.

To retreat to her satchel of medicines to prepare another batch of healing tea for him.

To hide her reaction to the feel of his skin beneath her fingers.

To hide her scarred face from his probing gaze.

"Don't you know? Warrior scars are a badge of honor."

"A badge of…" She sputtered at the absurdity. Yet memories returned of her father's men gathering in the great hall for a meal. The more seasoned among them bore the most scars, and none tried to hide the marks.

She turned to face him. "I'm not a warrior."

"Ye are." His brown eyes anchored her in place. "Ye hid the first two sisters and faced the soldiers bravely in the inn."

"Mayhap, but—"

"These new girls trust you because you've known their pain."

'Twas foolishness to believe that surviving Devlin's attack qualified her to lead anyone, let alone fight their battles. And yet, a part of her longed to be the woman she was born to be. To truly be the laird's daughter again.

While she'd never be able to go to the castle again, she could still lead her people in the wilderness. Her da would have liked that she hadn't given up completely on her heritage.

"You're their hero." Evan's quiet words sparked a hope that she quenched before it flamed into belief.

"Nay. Ye are the hero who made a difference." She waved a hand at the structure over their heads. "And as a friar, ye can…"

"I'm not truly a friar…"

Moira stepped back to take in the man before her from head to toe. Brown shapeless robe. Approachable countenance. *Not a friar?* His words contradicted everything she knew about the man. Well, except for that kiss. But surely a fever-induced moment of attraction meant little in the eyes of God and a man of the cloth.

He lowered his voice and his gaze. "Actually, I'm just a curious Sinclair who wanted to discover more about the Gunns before our clans united."

"Yer a…" Moira stared at the top of his head. Could it be that her foolish attraction wasn't sinful after all? That his sword-wielding protective strength could be admired without need for confession and penance?

The surge of relief that there could possibly be a future for the two of them disappeared with the uncomfortable realization that while he'd been sitting in the corner of the inn with a bowl of stew and listening to their tales, he'd been lying to all of them.

To her.

She might have good reason to hide her own identity, but what drove him to go to such lengths, masquerading as an impartial observer?

Moira lowered her voice to a hiss. "And just what have you discovered about us, oh master spy?"

Sincerity emanated from his eyes and voice to settle her uncertain heart. "That the Gunns...that ye...are a people worth protecting from yer own leader."

The fight drained from her shoulders as she recalled how much he'd already helped them.

She too had been curious about the Sinclairs. Where they lived and what sort of people they were. And if Evan were to be believed, justice would come to her people.

At least it would once Evan was strong enough to finish his journey back home.

She reached for the cup of tea and helped him sit enough so he could lean against her while drinking it. But their close proximity reminded her of his faint...and the brush of a kiss that preceded it.

Especially when his gaze dropped to her lips again.

She'd seen that look in a man's eyes before. A look that always twisted into disgust when they saw the rest of her face. With her hair still back in a braid and all her flaws exposed, Evan's continued interest didn't make sense.

Her stomach fluttered at the strange feelings his attention ignited. She wanted to hide, yet she also acknowledged a tug to tell him her secret too.

Could she trust him?

Nay. 'Twas too soon after his own admission of trickery to abandon her long habit of silence. But perhaps she could use this chance to satisfy her own curiosity.

"Tell me about the Sinclair holdings."

CHAPTER NINE

Evan settled against the pile of blanket-covered branches serving as his sick bed and watched Maggie try to cover her blush with a flurry of activity.

Other than a distant memory of Maggie cleaning his injury and a vague realization that the throbbing pain in his arm and head had eased, he had no idea how long he'd lain here. Had Maggie truly cared for him through an apparent sickness? Or was her whispering voice merely part of a dream?

With a raging thirst scratching in his throat, he reached for a nearby waterskin. Weakness left him unable to move as far as he needed to, so he let his empty hand drop beside him.

He wouldna be traveling anytime soon.

"Did ye forget yer home?" Maggie's arched eyebrow reminded him that he'd yet to answer her question. "Or 'twas that a lie too?"

A not-so-subtle dig at his earlier deception, but the stolen glances at his face while she helped him with the waterskin softened the criticism.

His bossy beauty was back.

And he was glad he'd told her the truth of his identity.

Mayhap he'd have a private moment later to explore the growing feelings that bound his heart to the woman before him.

He swallowed several times, then pushed the skin away. "I didna forget. Ye'd like where I grew up. We've a few forests like these but also vast plains of heather under big skies and coastal views of the endless sea crashing against the rugged cliffs."

"I've never seen the sea but have heard tales from those who travel the trade routes." She set the waterskin atop his chest where he could easily take more sips when he was ready.

"I ken of many who would welcome access to yer wildlife in exchange for smoked fish from the sea. An alliance 'twill be good for more than yer clan's safety." He frowned. If only they could talk of trade instead of protection from enemies both within and without.

"Which is yet another reason to get ye back on yer feet." Her frown matched his.

"Another? What be the first?"

"We need ye to go for help. For all of us." She waved a graceful hand at the clearing full of women. "And for our families."

With fresh eyes, he took in the finished improvements on the shelter, evidence they had been busy whilst he was abed.

He also caught the scent of roasting meat on the breeze and his mouth watered. "If'n ye need me back on me feet, do ye have anything I can eat?"

"Aye. Ye're much improved." She laughed. "I can almost hear yer stomach rumbling from here."

Which was a good sign even if he could scarcely stand on his own. "With good food and rest, I may be ready to make the trek the day after the morrow."

"We'll see. But first, let's get some meat into ye." Maggie helped him upright, then wrapped an arm about his waist to steady him as he gained his balance. Soon they staggered together into the clearing where the sunshine fell warm upon his face.

Relishing the feel of her body against his side, he leaned a bit more on her than necessary. The small curve of her waist fit within his hand as naturally as the hilt of his sword after years of practice. How empty he would feel without her once he returned alone to the Sinclair keep.

Her arm tightened around his waist, and he forced himself not to startle at the pressure. Could it be she needed the contact as much as he did? He pushed the thought from his mind. If only that were true.

'Twasn't long afore the others noticed them and swarmed around to help him sit on a log near the fire, plying him with their best wishes and prayers.

He exchanged a glance with Maggie. Should he tell the rest of them the truth?

She shook her head, then handed over an improvised plate with a scoop of porridge and a hefty chunk of roasted rabbit meat.

"Donna give me more than my fair share."

"I didna." She shrugged her shoulders and offered a shy smile. "I set the snares the way we did afore and caught several rabbits already. Plus the girls have already hooked a string of fish."

He nodded and dug into his meal.

Out of the corner of his eye he watched Maggie move among the others with an easy grace and somewhat regal posture. Along with a keen sense of natural leadership, she passed out compliments and instructions as easily as if she were born to the task.

Never afraid to bend her own back for a task like chopping firewood yet equally able to give the injured girls instructions that made them feel like an important part of the camp.

She was beautiful both inside and out.

As if sensing the direction of his thoughts, she glanced over at his seat beside the fire, then looked away with a blush rising on her cheeks.

He too shifted his attention to the surrounding woods lest someone else—or Maggie once more—find him with his eyes still on her, but his thoughts lingered on the mysterious maiden.

She was more than a mere Maggie.

While she might feel the same attraction growing between them, she'd also need time to adjust to his true identity.

And lack of church-servant status.

He frowned at the vague memory of her soft skin beneath his lips…while wearing the drab friar's robe. For heaven's sake, he was to be a man who had supposedly taken a vow of chastity.

No wonder she'd turned as skittish as a newborn colt.

'Twas a lot to adjust to, but combined with the odd conversation about her name he'd overheard back at the inn and the gap-riddled story she'd told him before they'd had to climb the tree, he sensed she held a few secrets of her own.

He needed to earn her trust. And for that, they needed to converse without fear of reprisal or discovery.

She'd obviously already mastered the snares, but they'd need more than rabbits and fish to feed this many mouths while also having enough left over to smoke for a future journey. Maybe tomorrow when he was stronger he could use hunting as an excuse to get Maggie alone.

Evan awoke before the rest of the camp with a clear head and a sense of purpose. Today he would hunt for meat and fish that should keep the women fed for the days ahead and the next he would strike out for home alone.

His eyes drifted across the clearing to the shelter where the others slept. He'd miss Maggie but would enjoy the time away from the rest of them. After Evan had earned their trust and they'd felt safe from harm within the boundaries of the clearing, quiet whispers had turned into endless chatter about gowns and lads and bairns. Leaving Evan with an aching head.

No wonder Maggie had silently warned him to keep his non-friar status a secret from the husband-hunters among them.

'Twas yet another reason he'd used his improving health—and their reputations—to move his bedding out of the shelter last eve. And once they awoke, he'd be eager to get away into the relative quiet of the woods again.

Almost as much as he wished to be free of the wretched robe.

In addition to being a constant reminder of his deceptive role, the garment stank and the bulky weight hindered his movements. Could he use the excuse of laundering it to change into the simple peasant's tunic and braies in his pack?

Surely the others could be practical about such matters since few carried extra garments themselves and several had already spent time near the creek, returning with clean hair and damp clothing.

His decision made, Evan retrieved the garments and a bar of lye soap before striding toward the creek for a much-needed scrub. While he'd prefer to wear the Sinclair plaid also stowed in the bottom of his pack, he'd be content with this first step away from his status as spy. Maggie might be accepting of his true identity, but the others would need time to adjust.

Time he didn't have.

By the time he'd returned from the creek carrying the sodden-but-clean robe, the rest of the camp had roused and a pot of an aromatic breakfast cooked over the fire. His stomach growled in anticipation but 'twas soon drowned out by girlish giggles and whispers as three of the women espied his changed appearance.

Their obvious glances at his bared legs made him uncomfortable beneath the attention his brother would have soaked up with pleasure. Nay. 'Twas only one woman he wished to impress.

He draped the robe across several bushes to dry, then ignoring their continued flirtatious glances, sought out Maggie instead. "I couldna stand the stench of myself, but I'm afraid I also washed away your hard work." He pointed to the open gash on his arm.

She smiled, then motioned him toward the shelter and her satchel of medicines. "It needed a fresh poultice anyway." Minutes later, her gentle fingers probed the edges of his tender wound. "'Tis healing at last but ye'll need to keep it clean and dry."

"Nay more baths or laundry then?"

"Or rainstorms either."

They shared a smile over their earlier adventures before she crushed the herbs and mixed them with water to form a paste. Her touch sent tingles of awareness skittering throughout his body as she packed the wound, then wrapped a clean strip of cloth the same color as her dingy gown over his arm.

Her peeks at the muscles in his legs and chest proved he wasn't the only one affected by their contact. He smirked. It seemed she liked him shed of the shapeless robe as much as he.

As she tied a knot to secure the bandage, he scrambled for a reason to linger. What was his mission for the day supposed to be? Oh right. Hunting.

After a minute of digging through their pile of belongings, he emerged with the bow and quiver of arrows. "Graham told me you also know how to use these."

Maggie turned from repacking her satchel. "'Tis been a while." She shook her head, but the spark in her eyes told a different story. "Ye should use them."

"Mayhap." He followed her to rejoin the others gathered around their morning meal, then took the chance to state his case publicly. "But ye'll need a refresher for when I'm gone. After we break our fast, show me where ye set the snares, and we can take a little target practice."

He let his gaze skim over the too-observant eyes of the other seven women. "While I wouldna have chosen to fall ill, ye have already shown ye can survive without me. All ye need now is a lot of meat—"

"Kill us a turkey or two and ye'll be the hero again." The outspoken redhead batted her eyes.

"'Tis not about being a hero." Even if he was flattered by the attention and the implied trust that he was up to the task.

Maggie coughed, the noise doing little to cover her laughter.

He frowned. "'Tis about having enough extra meat to smoke or dry. Ye canna stay here forever and will need food to carry with ye when the time comes."

A serious hush fell over the group. He turned to face Maggie and lifted the bow while the women considered his words.

She sighed, then nodded.

After a quick bite of porridge, they soon headed toward the creek. It didn't take long to check the snares, but after spotting a few markings on the opposite bank, he quickly helped Maggie across the water.

With a low voice, he pointed out the tracks of several large birds as well as a few deer, then softly trod farther into the woods with Maggie on his heels. At a rustle ahead, he lifted a hand to stop her progress, then notched an arrow to the bowstring.

A large turkey stepped into a clearing, another bird of equal size behind it. Evan let the first arrow fly and followed it a moment later with the second. Both birds dropped in a flutter of feathers, and he hurried to make sure they were dead before retrieving the arrows.

"So ye just had to be the hero, did ye?" Maggie's teasing brought a smile to his face, but the admiration shining in her eyes brought his heart to life.

Every man should be so lucky to have a woman like her beside him.

For the first time in his life, he was the strong one. The warrior who could conquer anything.

The man he was meant to be.

"If I promise not to faint this time, can I kiss ye for real?"

A blush spread across her face, but she didn't turn away.

He trailed a finger along her scar to rest under her chin before lifting her face to meet his. Without the fog of illness clouding his senses, he savored the contact, taking time to fully explore her soft lips with his. Lips that trembled then clung to his as she responded to his touch.

After lifting his head just enough to inhale her sweet breath, his mouth descended again for another taste as her arms wrapped around him. Finally coming up for air, he tucked her in close to his pounding chest with the growing conviction that this precious woman was everything he'd ever wanted in a mate. God had put him into her life when she'd needed him most, and that had to mean something.

Never mind that they came from different clans.

Or that his father might have a different plan when it came to forging the alliance.

Or that he still believed she held back something of her story.

They could figure out the details later, even if it took a lifetime.

He kissed the top of her head. "I ken 'tis much to be decided between our clans, but I'm stating it now. I want to marry ye and build our home beside the sea."

He bit his tongue as he awaited her response, his future hanging in the balance.

CHAPTER TEN

The steady beat of Evan's heart beneath her ear stilled Moira's reaction.

Clearly befuddled by the lingering tingle of his fingertip along her scar and the tenderness of his warm lips on hers, she clung to the anchor of his strength.

Relished the feel of his muscular frame surrounding and sheltering her.

But what had he said?

Marriage. To her. Offering a home with the Sinclairs.

The enticing temptation to have a simple life in a new place with the man of her dreams.

After all, the man who held her had proven himself to be a strong protector with an honest faith. Despite not being a true friar, one couldn't fake the sincerity of his prayers.

The swirl of thoughts she'd been unable to process while surrounded by the other girls settled into a steady assurance.

She loved this man.

"Ye'd be safe."

He offered a refuge away from Isla. But Moira wasna the only Gunn in peril.

She loosened her grip on his shirt-clad torso. "With Midsummer's Eve a mere sennight away, how long until the others are safe too?"

Evan hummed. "The party traveling to forge the alliance should be passing by in a few days. I'll have to rejoin my family before they get too far into Gunn land, but once I share what I've learned, their plans should change."

Instead of a wedding, those plans could now involve a war. She shivered.

He ran strong hands along her arms, then stepped back to stare into her eyes. "I'll definitely talk to my da about us and make him see things my way."

The party to forge the alliance would include the laird and his son. And if Evan could talk freely to both his da and his liege lord, then...

She remembered his story about visiting her family's home as a child and recalled the intricate carving on the sword he'd used to kill the boar.

The same detail graced the dagger at his belt.

Despite the simple clothes he now wore, this man was not a commoner with a simple life. Nor a friar dedicated to the church. He was part of the elite warriors who protected their laird. Who lived at a castle by the sea.

While her true home 'twas a different castle miles away from the Sinclair land. 'Twas impossible anything between them could come to be.

"We could even be married in a fortnight or two."

She stared at the man so out of reach. A man who believed her to be a kitchen maid or a serving wench.

He chuckled. "I can see I've stunned ye speechless. Take yer time while I dress these birds, but ken I'll do all I can to give ye a happy life."

The dream dangling before her eyes disappeared behind a cloud of reality, and a numbing shroud descended around her heart.

They had no hope of a future.

Evan might be able to overlook her scar but his family wouldn't. Nor his clan. He'd be expected to make a quality match, and she had nothing to bring to a marriage.

Especially when she was hiding the truth of who she was.

Of who she used to be.

Guilt ate at Moira's soul. He'd told her the truth about himself, but her silence continued her lie. Would he despise her when he learned the truth?

Not to mention, even if she wanted to marry him, she couldn't make that vow under her alias. She'd have to claim her true name and identity at the altar.

Maybe it was time to come back from the dead.

But then what?

Would Isla kill her for good? Would her people believe her story? But if she had the Sinclairs on her side...

"Will yer kinsmen really right her wrongs?" The question slipped out from between tight lips.

Evan glanced up from the half-plucked birds with a frown. "Donna fash yerself. They willna fall for her schemes after I convince them of the truth."

She nodded. 'Twas so hard to believe that after five long years her nightmare might soon be over.

"I should leave in the morning but I willna forget—"

"So soon?" How had she come to rely on his presence so quickly?

"I canna risk missing them on the road."

'Twas true. And more lives than hers lay in the balance.

"But ken that if I must, I'll personally take her down so she canna hurt ye again." The protective gleam in his eyes warmed her heart.

"Once she's gone, everything will change." Moira could come out of hiding. But who would lead her clan if she escaped to the sea?

Would her clan judge her as lacking? Would they believe she was another victim from Isla's reign of terror, or would some blame her silence for their current troubles? Could she have prevented the injuries to Finella and Akira?

And if she did take her rightful position, would the leaders of her clan marry her off to an unknown man from among the Sinclairs even if she hadn't been the one to request the alliance? She couldn't imagine marrying anyone other than Evan. But if she came forward—assuming she survived the revelation—she might not have a choice.

Did her duty lie with her kingdom…or her heart? If only her parents were alive for her to ask.

"What's troubling ye now?"

"There are consequences ye donna know about. Consequences I'm not sure—"

"Tell me."

"I'm not sure I can." Tears flooded her eyes at the thought of giving him up. "Not yet."

She might actually be safer hiding away from everyone's gossip and plans for her after all.

He blew out a frustrated breath, then sighed. "Ye'll tell me when ye're ready?"

"Aye." Relief at gaining time to think through the consequences of coming back from the dead faded at the realization that if she decided to deny his suit she might break his heart. Could she do that to him?

And after all he'd done for her—including truly see past her scars—she couldn't bear to let him go.

She simply had to let him think there was still hope, if only to restore the smile to his handsome face. She'd nurse her broken heart alone later.

Moira rested a hand on his shoulder. "I need some time to figure out how to make this—us—work once the battle is over."

A spark of hope lit in his eyes again.

"But I have to see to the girls' safety before I can think of my own future. We need to get this meat back to them so it can be preserved." She knelt beside the fowl and helped remove the feathers from the second bird. "Ye can even take some with ye when ye take yer stories back to yer people."

He removed the first bird's entrails with a grunt. "I'd like to bring back more than dead turkeys as proof of my adventures."

His eyes darted to her face and she leaned back. "Oh no. I won't be a spectacle."

"It's not that. At least not only that." His urgent voice lowered to a whisper. "You know what she's like. What her soldiers are like."

"But I'm needed here." 'Twas true enough, but even if 'twasn't, her heart might not survive more time together before having to let him go.

"If they have more than enough meat and provisions, will you come?"

While she might have denied the pleading in his voice, the longing in his eyes softened her resolve. "Mayhap. But only if I'm sure they'll be fine."

His eyes roamed her face, then settled on her lips. "I willna take nay for an answer."

Ready or not, she was being forced out of the shadows. Once anyone outside her remote village knew of her existence, the discovery of her true identity became inevitable.

Sparks of attraction rushed between them with the speed of a horse engaging in battle. Afore she could lodge another protest, Evan leaned toward her. She closed her eyes, readying herself for another kiss. A kiss she wanted. A kiss she *needed*. Just as his lips reached hers, a rustle in the undergrowth interrupted them and they broke apart.

He grabbed the bow beside him and notched an arrow as an enormous stag stepped into the clearing. A sure shot later and they had meat aplenty.

An answer to his prayer, not hers.

While working alongside Evan to butcher the animal and pile the meat onto the hide atop an improvised sled, her thoughts swirled. Fear for her life mixed with longing for a future with Evan only to be replaced by dread at letting him go for the sake of her people.

Almighty God, help me know what to do.

✳ ✳ ✳

Evan adjusted his grip on the slippery poles, then dragged the heavy load over the small rocks protruding from the moss. A sharp twinge in his right arm and the overall weakness in his limbs reminded him that he'd been abed with a fever just yesterday.

Just a little farther. As soon as they got this bounty back to camp, the other girls could take over the task and he would rest then.

With a grunt, he heaved the meat around a log and neared the bushes where Maggie waited.

His Maggie, with the bow and quiver slung over her slim shoulders…and the lingering mixture of longing, confusion, and fear in her deep violet eyes. If only she trusted him enough to share her true concerns. Or believed in his declaration of love enough to explain what she meant by consequences.

'Twas possible he'd been moving too fast or taking advantage of their unusual circumstances.

Mayhap she feared his interest would fade once he returned to his people. Yet he'd seen all the Sinclair lasses and none captivated his imagination or stirred his inner warrior like this one.

Truth be told, he'd lost his heart in just a few days. Yet he'd never been so certain of anything. Now he only needed the time to prove himself and fully win her trust.

He smiled and a rosy blush blossomed on Maggie's face before she turned to part the bushes ahead. A few steps later, he emerged from the shadowy woods and blinked in the brighter light beside the creek.

Almost as if he'd stepped out of the shadow of younger son into a new role as Maggie's God-ordained protector. With the added responsibility to watch over the rest of the girls too.

Mayhap 'twas time to leave the lies behind and step into the full light of truth as well.

Before that thought had time to take root, one of the younger girls fishing upstream spotted their approach and ran to fetch the others. It took multiple trips, but in time they carried the meat across the creek and back to camp.

Evan endured their teasing about not being content with two large birds, then raised his voice to be heard above the collective joy. "Excuse me. I ken there still be much to do with this bounty, but I need yer help."

He glanced at Maggie near the back of the group, then waited for the others to quiet. Watchful eyes trained on his, and his palms began to sweat. How would they take his story? "My full name is Evan Sinclair…and I'm not really a friar." He raised his hands for silence. "I adopted the disguise as a ruse to gather the truth about Isla and yer clan, but now I need to leave in the morning to get word to my kinsmen."

The boldest of the group stepped forward with a flirtatious smile that turned his insides into a cringe. 'Twas the risk he took to reveal his identity. "How can I help?"

"In addition to needing supplies for the journey, I'd also prefer to offer proof of Isla's actions."

From the back of the group, Maggie's quick gasp caught the others' attention.

If 'twasn't so critical a task, he wouldn't pressure her. "I'd like Maggie and Finella to be there when I talk to the leaders of my clan, and I understand, Finella, if'n ye feel better having your sister Jenna along. We've a day's walk ahead to the rendezvous point and may have a few more days to wait for them to arrive."

"What about their reputations? Traveling alone with ye since yer not really a friar." Birkita words were reasonable, but he'd caught the flash of jealousy in her narrowed eye, as if she were less concerned about propriety than about being left behind with the others.

"They won't be alone since we're traveling as a group." As much as he wanted a marriage with Maggie, he didna wish her forced into it because of a soiled reputation.

"And what about the rest of us while yer gone?" As the smallest of the girls voiced her concern, others nodded.

He waved a hand at the pile of venison. "Ye'll have plenty of food to eat for days to come. And I promise to send the lasses back with a few trusted men to serve as protectors and guides to reunite ye with yer families."

After a few minutes of heated discussion, the group latched onto the hope being offered and embraced his plan. They spent the remainder of the day slicing, roasting, drying, and smoking meat aplenty for both the main camp and the traveling group to carry with them.

At dusk, he gathered Maggie and the other two. "Pack lightly, then get yer rest. We leave at dawn."

* * *

Two days after departing for Sinclair land, Evan chafed at the sense his time with Maggie was running out. Sitting around their camp with nothing to do should have been the ideal opportunity to talk, but it hadna worked out like he'd hoped.

When they'd first reached the road on the border between the Gunn and Sinclair lands, scouting for signs of a group's passing had occupied him. Once he'd ensured he and the women were safe from violent soldiers, he'd focused on building yet another shelter.

But with those tasks done and a large supply of meat in their packs, he didn't even have an excuse to go hunting. Instead, he was doomed to lean against a large rock and sneak glances at the woman who had captured his heart while she sat on a log beside their fire ring and stared into the distance with only her thoughts for company.

She'd uttered barely a word since he'd shot the stag, but a bevy of emotions flitted across her face. At times it seemed like she was about to say something, only to retreat as their vigilant chaperones filled the silence with oft-meaningless chatter.

While he hoped she would eventually give a positive response to his awkward—mayhap presumptuous—proposal, there were times she watched him as if judging his trustworthiness. That is, when she wasn't sneaking peeks at his attire.

Discarding the peasant clothes and donning a nicer tunic along with his family plaid had been a statement of identity. 'Twas who he was born to be, and she'd need to come to terms with it.

Evan could appreciate her caution but longed for resolution between them. For another chance to convince her of his return.

Mayhap even a chance for another kiss.

Because once his family arrived, he would be whisked away to help plan and execute their strategy for saving the Gunn clan from their erratic leader. While the lasses would be on their own again.

He cleared his throat. "Do ye remember how to get back to the others?"

"Aye." Jenna rolled her eyes with a grumble. "Ye've told us over and over. Nay more."

Finella nudged Maggie. "Go talk to him afore he explodes. Put the man out of his misery."

Evan choked back a laugh. Were his feelings so obvious?

Maggie's cheeks turned pink, but she rose and headed toward the side of the road.

He whispered a thank ye to the other girls, then turned his back on their knowing smiles to follow after Maggie.

Once they were alone in the shade of a few trees, he lifted her chin with a gentle finger and stared into her eyes. "I ken ye're worried, but I promise I'll come find ye when the battle is over."

Her eyes drank in his words but still held a hint of doubt. As if she were afraid to hope. Afraid to fully trust his word.

How could he convince her?

He propped his hands on his tartan-clad hips, his fingers brushing against the dagger hanging from his belt. Without hesitation, he removed the leather sheath and held out the weapon before him. "This was my mother's. Ye keep it for now as a pledge. I *will* be back to claim it...and you."

She reached for the gift with trembling hands, then sighed. With a lift of her chin, resolve filled her eyes. "Ye've probably already guessed, but I've been doing a lot of thinking these past few days."

The precious sound of her voice soothed the parched places in his soul and brought a smile to his face.

"I'm not who ye think." The whispered confession hung between them like the morning mist over a loch.

His heart raced. At last, it seemed she trusted him enough to tell the truth.

Her voice cracked. "And I donna ken what to do. But mayhap if I share the burden ye can help—"

The sound of thundering hooves on the road had him shoving her behind him and drawing his sword. While the riders approached from the direction of the Sinclair keep, until he could be certain Maggie remained safe, he would take no chances that other clansmen approached from his family's land.

As the first riders neared, the familiar colors eased his mind. After sheathing his sword, he stepped out onto the road and waved them to a stop.

In the midst of the milling horses, his father nudged his mount to the front, then raised his eyebrows. "How'd ye get here so fast and where's yer horse?"

His chest tightened at the proof his father hadn't noticed his absence over the past week...or during their current trip.

Donald's black beast sidled up. "Ah, the prodigal has been found." His brother sneered. "Ye'd be late to yer own wedding."

A few of the older warriors added their own good-hearted jabs. Nothing he hadna heard before, but with Maggie listening, he felt more foolish than heroic.

For her sake, he squared his shoulders and raised his voice. "Ye'll be glad I came ahead of ye, because I'm not sure 'twill be a wedding. Not after ye hear what I've learned."

His father's man-at-arms drew his sword as if to punish Evan for his insolence, but was stopped by his laird, who slowly dismounted. "Let's hear what the lad has to say."

At a rustle behind him, he glanced over his shoulder to see that the other girls had joined Maggie beneath the tree.

Time to face the gauntlet and present the truth.

"Sure hope the rest of the Gunn lasses are better looking that these hideous ones Evan's been keeping company with." He'd know his brother's voice—and insults—anywhere and cringed as some of the men laughed.

He blistered his clansmen with a glare and strode toward his father with clenched fists. "Laugh now, but the madwoman ye wish to align with caused their wounds."

CHAPTER ELEVEN

M oira caught her breath.

She should be used to the taunts by now. After all, this group of Sinclairs on horseback weren't the first men to think her hideous.

'Twas, however, the first such rejection for Finella. Moira pushed the girl behind her and glared at the instigator of the ridicule. "Never mind the louts. Ye're yet healing and the honeyed salve is doing its work."

The other lass sniffed behind her. "Aye. But they shouldna say such things about ye either."

"Mayhap." But they had and her only defense was to pretend it didna matter.

If only she'd worn her hair down to cover her face.

And if only Evan hadn't left her standing alone and vulnerable by the side of the road when he'd stopped the Sinclairs and approached their leaders.

Her eyes strayed from the laughing men to her hero. A man who'd also been mocked by his clansmen for losing his horse when he'd deliberately left it behind in order to help them with their escape. He didna deserve their jests any more than Finella did.

He'd protected them from harm, built a shelter while barely able to stand, supplied them with meat, and even now kept his promise to relay the truth to his clan.

Her gaze drifted over the other warriors surrounding their leader. They too stared but with different eyes. Questioning eyes. As if they wondered what caused her and Finella's injuries. A few even cringed, hinting that perhaps they understood the pain they had endured.

The initially curious expressions turned grim.

The truth Evan shared indeed carried weight, and with their visible injuries as proof of Isla's devious intentions and cruel behavior, Moira's people now had an ally in the Sinclairs—just not in the way Isla intended.

Justice would be done.

Yet would these same men look at her now with pity? Would they find her lacking and try to convince Evan to look elsewhere for a bride?

She couldn't bear his desertion, not after he was the first man since Graham to treat her as someone worthy of love.

Glancing back to the man who held her heart, she discovered that he now argued with the Sinclair laird. Nearby stood the mocking young warrior who strongly resembled both men.

Almost as if…

Evan had said he needed to talk to his father. Others had joked about him being late to his wedding. Almost as if he were the one marrying a Gunn woman to forge the alliance between the clans. If so, then he was not a mere man-at-arms but an heir.

Nay wonder he'd felt the need to get more information about her clan afore saying his vows.

And yet, while she hadn't known the full extent of his identity, he knew who he was. And he had still wanted to build a future with her.

With his support, maybe she really could start over in a new land where people saw her scar as a sign of being a survivor.

STEPPING INTO THE LIGHT

And if she came back from the dead to take her proper place within her clan, who better to forge the alliance than her? She would marry Evan as an equal, knowing he loved her for her heart—despite her scars—and not merely for her name or position.

One of the warriors separated from the heated discussion in the middle of the road and approached them. He skirted past Moira to study Finella with her fresh burns. "The young Sinclair tells quite a tale, but I'd like to hear it from yer own lips."

* * *

Evan stood his ground while his father lectured him for pulling another stunt and having a flair for the dramatic. Nothing he hadna heard before.

In the past 'twas his only way to gain attention. And now with Maggie likely hearing everything that was said, the criticism stung. But he knew the truth.

This time 'twas about taking a stand. To fight for the defenseless. To be the man he now knew God had created him to be.

He lifted his chin and stared at the circle of his father's best warriors. "What do ye truly ken about Isla?"

The multiple voices overlapped as they told the tale of a grieving twice-widowed woman who had recently lost her only child.

"She's been regent since her son Roan was young and remains so after his death."

"Aye. Lady Isla's only doing what's best fer her clan."

"Nay. Don't call her a lady." Evan raised his voice to silence the lies. "She only does what's best for her. Did ye not see the lasses? Isla did this to them. And there are still more hiding in the woods because their families fear for their lives should they be called to the castle."

His father frowned, then motioned Quinn, his second-in-command, closer. "Confirm the story and see to their needs." After the man left, the Sinclair laird focused his full attention on Evan. "Tell me all ye've learned."

Evan relaxed his stance, thankful for his father's attention but wary nonetheless from years of the man's disinterest in him. "I only meant to listen to the gossip and return unnoticed afore the group left our keep, but I couldna turn my back on their need." He started his report with the villagers' legend of Angus Gunn's mystery illness, his daughter's disappearance into the woods, his death, and Isla's reign for the last five years.

When he reached the part about the Matheson sisters rushing into the inn and the villagers collectively hiding them from Isla's soldiers, more Sinclair warriors gathered closer to listen. He moved the tale from their initial journey to the cave then on to the second camp where they met up with lasses from two other villages, including the girl with the fresh burns and another who had been badly beaten. "They needed someone to protect them."

His brother chuckled. "And even ye'll do in a pinch."

"Enough." Their father frowned at Donald before turning back to Evan. "And their leader? The one with the braid and deep scar on her face?"

"I donna ken her full story yet, but she goes by the name Maggie. She was the first one injured, years ago. Long afore an alliance by marriage was suggested." Evan smiled at the thought of her. "Speaking of which, I know Donald's wedding would matter most, but if an alliance with their clan is still possible, I wish to support the merge…with Maggie as me bride."

His brother's face twisted in disgust, but his father looked thoughtful for a change.

"Why do ye think Isla would hurt her own people?" One of the other warriors watched Evan with sincerity in his eyes. Perhaps he had a chance at convincing this group of warriors to take him seriously after all.

"The villagers I overheard think 'tis jealousy and that mayhap she's seeking to forge her third marriage with another laird to secure her future. That she's eliminating the competition so she seems the better option."

His father shuddered. "So if we canna trust Isla, what do we do now?"

An argument ensued between those wishing to simply walk away from the alliance and others seeking to bring justice and protect the innocent Gunn people.

"Aye, there needs to be an alliance for the clan's sake else some other vulture swoops in."

Evan cleared his throat. "I also heard that a Sutherland messenger was seen around the castle. She could be courting both sides or have a double cross in mind."

"I donna believe she'd be that devious." His father crossed his arms over his chest. "But 'twould be wise to exercise caution else we walk into a trap."

"We wouldna be approaching the castle unassisted." Evan eyed his father's advisers, then relayed what he'd learned about Finella's father and his quest to rally the clan at the upcoming celebration. "They hope the Sinclairs will act on their behalf, but if not, they're preparing to act on their own. But 'twould be a slaughter since they are ill-equipped to lay seige to the stronghold."

The Sinclair warriors' shocked faces at a clan choosing to revolt against their leader soon turned to stone. To make a stand against such odds spoke only of extreme desperation.

And called to the Sinclair clan's vow to uphold justice.

His father nodded. "What do ye ken of their stronghold and its defenses?"

Tension drained from his shoulders. The lines were drawn and the Sinclairs would side with the common people.

Maggie would soon be safe.

* * *

Moira bit back a smile as the Sinclair warrior's scowl deepened further than the ravine that bordered the Gunn keep.

Finella's story of broken promises and being tripped into the fire culminated with the tale of Akira's beating when she'd refused to step forward as Isla's next victim. Followed by their father's plan to send the village daughters into hiding while the men gathered their clan's support.

"And what be yer story? When were ye wounded?" The warrior turned his attention to her.

"Five years ago." Moira swallowed the memories and chose merely to summarize. "The man who held his dagger to my throat said 'twas by Isla's order." Her hand swept up to indicate the path of the blade. "'Twas a foiled attempt at murder."

Jenna gasped and clutched her sister's hand while the warrior crossed himself as if warding off a curse.

He shook his head. "She would murder a child? She doesna deserve to live."

Evan had been right about his clan. When given the truth, they would defend and protect the innocent.

"Outside of the two of ye, are there other survivors?"

Survivors. *I'm a survivor.* Moria's nerves settled like the honey that had soothed Finella's raw skin. The confirmation that she'd overcome such a challenge and was included with the others as if she were worth protecting too filled her with hope.

She exchanged a glance with Finella. "Akira, the woman who was badly beaten, is recovering at our camp with other lasses who are in hiding rather than get taken to the keep. And I heard a story from the tanner in our village who recently traveled with a girl who was retrieved by her family but refused to speak of what happened during her stay. I donna ken where she lives."

The warrior nodded. "How many are at yer camp? And do ye need anything?"

"We left five behind including the other injured woman. Thanks to Evan's hunting we've plenty of meat but could use more grain for porridge." She glanced at Finella's healing burns. "And more honey to resupply my medicinal supplies if ye have any."

The man pivoted and motioned two other soldiers to join them.

While he gave the men instructions to protect and escort the women back to their camp, Moira realized the other Sinclairs showed no signs of lingering. In fact, she caught snippets and rumblings of a coming battle rather than a wedding. The truth about Isla's rule had come to light and the Sinclair plans for Midsummer's Eve had changed.

While part of her rejoiced that a battle would be fought on the Gunns' behalf, another chafed to be left behind. To be left out of the planning. As if she deserved a voice.

After the apparent captain of the guard returned to his laird's side, their appointed escorts excused themselves to gather provisions. As they strode to the back of the Sinclair group where a supply wagon had just arrived, she noticed the presence of a robed churchman and her heart thundered in her chest.

Could it be?

It was. Near the back of the traveling party, sat Father Tomas.

The priest from her youth slid from his horse and fell to his knees. With wide eyes fixed upon her face, he too made the sign of the cross.

His face paled almost as if he'd seen a ghost.

She waved a hand to acknowledge him—to acknowledge that his eyesight was true—then turned away with the growing realization that her secret 'twas as good as told. While she'd been prepared to reveal the truth to Evan and seek his wisdom, being recognized by yet another person sealed her fate.

She couldn't stay in hiding.

Prepared or not, 'twas time to shoulder the burden of her rightful identity and accept her future within her clan.

Moira took a deep breath and addressed the other girls. "Once our escort returns, we need to hurry back to camp.

Despite what the warriors may say, we won't be staying there. We need to spread the word to our families and the other villages that the Sinclairs are about to deliver justice." A righteous fire burned inside her chest. "It's time to stand together as a clan."

Finella nodded. "What about the other girls within the castle gates? And the servants?"

"We'll get word to them that they need to find a reason to leave before the battle."

"But who's going to listen to us?" Jenna glanced between them. "We're just a bunch of frightened girls."

"Nay." She sucked in another deep breath for courage. It was time. Time to be brave. Time to be truthful. "My name isn't Maggie. It's Moira. And like I told the Sinclair captain..." She pointed to her scar. "This happened when Isla had one of her soldiers try to kill me in the woods the day I turned a half score and three. Just a week afore my father, Laird Angus, succumbed to his illness. I've been in hiding ever since."

Finella gasped. "Ye looked familiar but I'm sorry, all I could see was the scar."

Moira squeezed Finella's uninjured shoulder. "As someone wise recently told me, scars are a badge of honor. They show we survived the battle when others weren't as lucky. We lived to fight another day." She eyed both girls with a new sense of resolve. "Like the seasoned warriors on the road beside us, we are warriors in our own right."

Their assigned escorts chose that moment to return, leading a few extra horses. Good. 'Twould make for faster travel both today and in the days to come.

Moira shot one last glance over her shoulder at Evan before turning toward her future.

'Twas time to rally the clan around her.

✳ ✳ ✳

Evan watched as Quinn returned to his laird's side. In a few quick statements the warrior relayed the stories of both girls and confirmed that the villagers planned to rally their clan together. Isla's treatment of the females in the Gunn clan had indeed ignited a fiery disgust in the eyes of all the men circling their laird. His clan had indeed reacted the way he'd known they would.

"I've sent two men to see the rest of the girls to safety. They'll rejoin us at the Gunn keep once their task is done." Quinn eyed his comrades and laird. "Now, when do we oust the villainous Isla and her minions?"

"Soon." Evan's father's half-smile revealed his approval for his second-in-command's passion for justice. The nod that followed set their official course. "And we'll show her the same mercy she showed the innocent."

"So, what's the plan?" Donald's voice cut into the gathering, sparking a rowdy discussion about battles and vengeance.

"And once the Gunns are freed from Isla's rule, what of the alliance then?"

"They'll need to appoint a new leader to speak on their behalf."

"But after we help them, they should be so grateful that they'd be happy to forge the alliance."

"But first, we take down the wicked witch."

Evan nudged closer to his father. "This isna the place to make proper plans for a battle, but there's a small village and inn little more than a half-day's ride up the road."

"And?" For the first time in his life, it seemed his father actually sought his counsel.

With a new warmth burning around his heart, Evan stood taller. "We'll need to stop for the evening. And even if Isla's soldiers still be lurking about, 'twould be logical for a Sinclair wedding party to stop for a proper meal." He shrugged. "'Tis a celebratory journey after all, and appearances will keep Isla unawares of our intent."

His father nodded. "And ye know this place because…"

"'Tis where I met Maggie and the first two girls. I left my horse in the care of the innkeeper, and I'm sure he'll be more than happy to give ye privacy for planning…and any additional information ye desire."

The firm hand clasped on his shoulder was all the reward his heart needed.

The Sinclair Laird raised a hand for silence. "Men, prepare to continue our journey to a place my son has found. Tonight we make our plans."

As Evan turned from the meeting, he spotted the girls disappearing into the woods with two of his father's trusted soldiers. They'd be well cared for.

He already missed Maggie's smile, but the sooner they did battle, the sooner they could be reunited.

After retrieving his pack from the abandoned campsite, he hurried toward the rear of the party to claim one of the spare horses such a large group always traveled with. Halfway there, he ground to a stop at the clan's priest frantic waving. 'Twas unusual for a man of the cloth to be associated with soldiers, but with the clan's original intention of attending a wedding, the priest's presence among the Sinclair warriors was easily explained.

Would Father Tomas continue with their party once he learned they were preparing for battle instead?

"What do ye know of the girl ye were with? The one with the scar?" A strange light glinted in the man's eyes.

Why the sudden curiosity? Except…ah yes. The priest had served the Gunn clan some time ago.

"She goes by the name Maggie, although I've yet to discover the full of her story. I came across her in a village where she'd been staying with the couple who took care of her after her injury."

"I'd like to meet them." Tears shimmered in the priest's eyes.

"Ye will. We're stopping there tonight." Evan nodded at the man bringing him a horse. "Since our plans have changed, mayhap ye can stay with them for a while."

"Mayhap." The priest's voice held more than a fair share of curiosity.

"I need to make sure they are unharmed. They're Maggie's only family."

At least until the battle was over and he could claim her as bride.

CHAPTER TWELVE

Evan whispered encouragement to his horse as the procession of Sinclairs began their final ascent to the Gunn fortress situated in the middle of the rocky slope.

Like his memory recalled and Graham's drawing confirmed, the steep hillside provided a natural defense to the south and west of the keep while rugged cliffs rose behind the stone stronghold. The wooded area to the east of the curtain wall ended in the deep ravine that fed into the loch they'd passed not a half hour ago.

In keeping with the plans forged two days prior around a table at Maggie's parents' inn, the Sinclairs would maintain the pretense of a peaceful group come to finalize the alliance arrangements as if intending to celebrate Midsummer's Eve a few days later with a wedding or two.

Whatever it took to peaceably get inside the castle gates.

His thoughts drifted back to Maggie's loyal guardian Graham. After Evan's father had peppered the man for details about the Gunn keep and situation, Graham had only enough time to give Evan a nod of approval before disappearing into a corner to talk to Father Tomas.

While he'd wished to be a part of that conversation in order to glean more of Maggie's history, Evan had instead endured hours of interrogation as he tapped into the depths of his childhood memories to determine the interior layout of the Gunn defenses, bailey, and keep.

At least whenever he saw her next, he'd be able to tell Maggie that the couple had been unharmed while she'd been hidden away in the wilderness.

As they bypassed a cluster of Gunn clan tents outside the castle walls, Evan forced a carefree smile to his face, then turned to crack a joke with his brother. 'Twould be a good reminder to the rest of the group of their roles in this façade—the Sinclairs were merely a happy group along to pick a few brides and enjoy the feast with an abundance of ale. Out of the corner of his eye, Evan saw that the supply wagons and a contingent of the trailing Sinclairs had separated from the main group. Their task was to make a show of setting up a camp outside the walls alongside of the Gunn clan members who had already gathered to bless the crops and beasts on the longest day of the year.

Those Sinclairs lingering outside the castle walls would not only surround the area but subtly offer their support to any of the Gunn clan members who had gathered in opposition to Isla.

Meanwhile, the main group now approached the open gates. Evan lifted his eyes to the tops of the walls looming overhead as if merely curious, but knew he wasn't the only Sinclair counting the number of guards.

Isla's hirelings, dressed in their distinctive red tunics, were easy to spot above the gray stone ramparts. However, Evan would have to get closer to the guards to identify the specific individuals who had tormented the innocent at the inn and then searched through the woods.

His insides clenched with the need to pursue justice. Scarface—Devlin—the captain of Isla's guard and the one who had hurt Maggie, would be his primary target.

Evan took a deep breath and forced his hands to relax on the reins as they proceeded through the gates, but upon reaching the upper bailey, a sense of unease settled upon his shoulders. For being so close to a major clan festival, only a handful of servants or crofters scurryied about. The scarcity of innocents afoot could signal a trap.

He glanced at his father, who simply nodded. The Sinclairs were prepared and watchful.

At the top of the stone steps leading up to the impressive keep a heavy oak door crashed open. A beautiful older woman stepped out, flanked by two red-shirted soldiers. Her lavish gown of golden silk accentuated her figure, and she'd left her dark hair to flow free, with only a thin circlet of gold at her crown holding the locks away from her face.

Could be none other than Isla. Her flawless appearance made it difficult to believe her capable of cruelty. Or deception.

Except he'd seen the evidence firsthand.

Once she had everyone's attention, she took a step forward and extended her arms. "Laird Sinclair, we welcome ye and yer handsome son as well as yer kinsmen. Please join me inside for a wee bit of refreshment after yer journey." Her eyes roamed the nearly vacant bailey. "Alas, it seems most of the lasses to be considered for a match have chosen this day to visit their families outside the gates."

She didna seem too disappointed to be the lone woman to greet the Sinclair contingent. Despite her smile, the lack of warmth in her eyes sent shivers down Evan's spine and he slipped back into the cluster of other Sinclair soldiers. For once he was glad to be overlooked.

After the group dismounted, a few of the Sinclair warriors led the horses toward the stables while others wandered about as if stretching their legs. Evan trailed the smaller contingent of his father's most trusted men inside the keep to the great hall.

Similar to their home near the sea, the common gathering space boasted a large fireplace at one end, scattered long tables for meals, and a rush-strewn stone floor. The abundance of wall-mounted torches offered little light to see by, and it took several moments for his eyes to adjust to the dimness of the hall.

As his father and brother took their places of honor at the raised head table, their men positioned nearby, Evan headed across the large room toward the door a serving girl had disappeared through. A door he remembered from his youth.

'Twas time to warn the castle staff.

When he finally reached the bustling hub of activity in the kitchens, a stout woman looked up from stirring a bubbling pot. Her eyes dropped to his plaid and she nodded with a slight tilt to her lips. "'Tis time."

Time to feed the visitors a light meal or time to bring justice? Both were true.

He nodded in return. "Aye."

The cook straightened, then raised her voice to be heard above the chatter. "Be alert, me lasses. We're not alone anymore."

Mayhap another double meaning lay within her words.

Evan followed the servants carrying trenchers of roasted mutton, tankards of ale, and a pitcher of wine to the Great Hall. Stopping near the attached buttery, he leaned against the stone wall.

A curious onlooker might think he was only interested in one of the serving wenches or in tasting the food, but his position would cut off a possible avenue for an attack...or escape.

All that remained was to wait for the signal from his kinsmen.

* * *

Moira huddled in the bushes outside the castle walls.

Ignoring her haunted memories from the last time she'd been in these verra woods, she focused her gaze on the stone fortress. 'Twas difficult seeing her beloved home again without grieving for all she had lost, but this battle would surely be worth it if the Sinclairs helped bring down Isla.

Rustling in the undergrowth nearby shifted her focus to the others encircling the keep. Many of the villagers held primitive weapons taken from the blacksmith's shop, but a few of her father's former knights had joined their ranks, including Dungald, the loyal yet since-demoted captain of the guard who had pledged his sword on her behalf.

Just one look at her face had convinced the knights of her identity…and their true loyalty.

While she should have come forward with the truth years ago, these brave men stood a far better chance of success now with the aid of the Sinclair warriors.

Their large traveling party had arrived a half hour ago but while a smaller contingent had entered the castle gates, many had remained outside the walls. On the surface, it appeared they were merely setting up camp for themselves, but she saw they had claimed critical positions to protect the tents of her clansmen while also cutting off escape routes.

A prickle of anticipation skittered across her skin as several of the Sinclairs casually wandered toward the gates as if stretching their legs. 'Twould not be long now.

Having done all she could to warn those inside to protect themselves, they could now only wait for whatever the Sinclairs had planned. Her people were simply there to prevent Isla and her guards from escaping the castle walls, especially out the side gate. There would be no refuge for them in the woods.

A strident hunting horn blew three long blasts that ricocheted off the stone walls.

Moira gripped Evan's dagger in her hand as the distinct sounds of clashing swords and warrior yells filtered out from within the walls. A minute later, more fighting erupted outside the walls and out of sight far to her left.

She fingered the pouch of herbs at her waist.

Almighty God, keep them—Evan—safe, especially since his sword arm is still healing. May I not have many injuries to treat when this is over.

125

Afore long only Sinclairs positioned themselves atop the walls and manned the gates with not a red-shirted Gunn in place. Their ally seemed to have caught Isla's guard by surprise.

A flash of red to her right caught her attention as several of Isla's guards rushed through the side gate, still glancing over their shoulders at the battle they fled.

Like the cowards they were.

With a shout, her clansmen descended to quickly surround and subdue them.

The grounds outside the keep, it seemed, were secure, but only Heaven knew what had happened inside its walls.

CHAPTER THIRTEEN

A fter the trumpet sounded, several of Isla's guards had left the hall to investigate.

However, the lady of the hour had stayed calm—or at least pretended to—and even waved Evan's father and brother back into their seats. "Whatever the trouble is, 'twill soon be over. After all, canna yer men see to yer safety?"

His father exchanged a glance with Donald, but resumed sitting. "Our men are more than capable of the task."

"'Tis good to hear." Isla reached for a nearby pitcher to refill their goblets. "Shall we drink to the new alliance?"

Evan narrowed his eyes and pushed away from the wall. She played at something.

A nearby serving wench with an armload of trenchers shoved against the head table, knocking the pitcher from Isla's hands. "Donna drink it."

Isla rose and turned on the servant with a vicious slap. "Ye clumsy oaf, begone at once."

"Nay." The girl straightened. "For Moira's sake, I'll not be letting ye poison them with yer words…or yer wine."

Evan drew his sword and backed the closest guard toward his mistress while his father, brother, and their men took advantage of the same distraction to disarm the remainder of Isla's guard.

Isla's guards couldn't hide their surprise and the sudden change of power, but did not appear afraid of their fate. Nor did the elegant woman seem at all concerned to have members of another clan holding her at sword point.

Perhaps they knew something the Sinclairs did not...

The heavy door to the outside burst open and Quinn rushed inside wielding his claymore. The warrior's eyes flickered across the Sinclair swords holding the Gunns at bay before he slowed his pace and lowered his sword with a slight smile. "My laird, the gates and walls are secured. There was also a small skirmish with a Sutherland scouting party who were hiding in the woods to the south of the keep. At the sound of the horn, they emerged, but were vanquished with ease."

Isla gasped and fear crept into the eyes of the other captives. As if the presence of the Sutherlands was less of a surprise than their defeat.

The Sinclair captain chuckled. "A few of the traitors tried to escape through a side gate, but the Gunns stopped them. Rumor has it that Moira has returned from the dead."

"Impossible." Isla startled, then sagged back in her chair, a hand fluttering across her chest. "Nay. He slit her throat and left her for the wild animals, just like I ordered. And with Angus weakened by his grief, 'twas easier for me to snuff out his last breath."

Had the woman just confessed to murdering the previous laird? Her own husband?

And this Moira? Strands of her story tugged at the fringes of his memory.

With wide eyes filled with the panicked fear of a cornered animal, Isla reached for something at her waist.

Evan shoved aside the only man standing in his way and pushed toward her to prevent a thrown dagger only to see her transfer something from the small pouch on her belt up to her mouth.

A moment later, violent convulsions threw her from her chair, and foaming spittle flew from her lips.

He stopped in shock, his sword wavering at the unexpected turn of events.

Obviously she'd ingested a lethal herb of some sort.

But why carry it on her person? Unless she'd truly meant to poison—or even kill his family—just like the servant had implied.

Truly she was a madwoman.

Before the final spasm ended her life, Isla's henchmen had surrendered their arms and were pushed into a corner where they could be kept under guard.

A Gunn manservant rushed forward from the shadows, waving an opened scroll. "Laird Sinclair, ye need see this."

A moment later his father threw the missive onto a nearby table. "The vile Sutherland laird had promised her a reward—and protection—if she could kill both me and me son." His eyes darted from Donald to Evan, then to the body lying on the rush-strewn floor.

Stunned that even the Sutherlands did not care to acknowledge his existence, Evan realized a moment later the depths of Isla's scheme.

Not only had she lured the Sinclairs to her hall with the promise of an alliance, only to attempt to serve them a drink laced with poison, the scouting party his kinsmen had vanquished from the woods had apparently been there to confirm the conclusion of the deed. They'd likely thought the horn was sounded to rally the Sinclairs after news that their laird was dead.

If curiosity hadn't sent him ahead of his kinsmen to seek out the truth, his family could be the ones lying motionless at his feet. Rage coursed through his veins at the treachery until he wished Isla were still alive so he could run a sword through her.

His father recovered from the turn of events faster than Evan and the others. With shouted orders echoing throughout the hall, he sent warriors to secure their defenses and round up the remainder of Isla's guards for questioning.

Unable to stomach another minute near the evidence of Isla's actions, Evan sheathed his sword and strode toward the opposite side of the hall. He'd check over the dead bodies to make sure all the culprits were accounted for. Later.

Before he could do anything else, he needed to calm himself.

Inhaling and exhaling slow breaths settled his racing heart and allowed clear thoughts to filter through his mind. His father and brother were safe. Isla was dead. Her confession paired with the missive from the Sutherlands damned her loyal soldiers and would make the coming trials short.

The remainder of the Gunns, including his precious Maggie, were now safe to live under the protection of the Sinclairs.

The tension draining from his shoulders, Evan spotted the tapestries adorning the wall, including those hanging outside the second-floor landing visible over the balcony. Using the excuse that he should check for additional guards elsewhere, he studied the various pieces of embroidery up close. Many seemed to be portraits of former Gunn lairds and their families while a few appeared to document other memorable events from their clan history.

As he followed the gallery up the stairs, the rich colors of thread brought back memories of his mother stitching beside the fire in the Sinclair keep's hall.

Maybe someday Maggie could sit in that same spot and stitch a tapestry of their family. Assuming that she finally told him—

Evan's eyes flickered over the next tapestry, then snapped back to stare at the vivid, unmistakable, violet-blue eyes of the young girl woven in place beside her parents.

An older version of the imp who'd trailed him during his earlier visit to the keep…and a younger version of the woman who'd captured his heart in the woods.

How could he not have seen the similarities sooner?

Like he'd thought, she was more than a mere Maggie.

She was Moira, the missing daughter of the last Gunn laird. A woman with a strong bloodline who fought to protect her people.

Evan braced a hand against the stone wall as he replayed every conversation, searching for clues that might have hinted to her past. From her fear that she'd be killed if she returned home to her belief that Isla acted out of jealousy, she'd told the truth while guarding her identity.

Yet the clues were there for those willing to see.

No wonder Father Tomas had asked such pointed questions about her. He'd been the priest here during her youth.

Moira. He tasted her name upon his lips and could almost recall the taste of their kisses.

Moira.

Now that she was safe from Isla, she'd be free to marry.

His smile faded. But if she was the heiress of this clan, Donald might try to marry her instead. And their father might approve.

He could not bear to watch the woman he loved wed to another.

From the great hall below, a whisper of excitement traveled his way, and Evan glanced over the balcony railing in time to see Moira step inside. A few of her Gunn clansmen trailed behind her, including both Finella and her sister.

He descended the step and rounded the corner into the hall in time to hear her ask for the Sinclair laird's heir.

His brother.

Evan stepped out of sight and leaned against the wall, bracing himself against the familiar sense of rejection.

More snippets of previous conversations came rushing back including her cryptic comments about consequences she couldn't talk about. About making sure the others were taken care of before she could think about her own future.

Having been raised with the motto of *clan before self*, he knew that duty required that she must ensure the survival of her clan before she considered her own wishes. In fact, he'd seen her struggle for several days to make a decision and knew the pain it caused her.

If her clan's survival required forging an alliance by marriage, the woman he loved would sacrifice her future for the sake of others.

Just like he must sacrifice his own to honor her choice. He drew a deep breath as his heart splintered within his chest.

No matter. He would fulfill his promise. She was home and he'd make sure she was safe, starting by securing her borders.

If only their personal desires aligned with their obligations to both of their clans.

* * *

Moira's eyes swept the rapidly-filling great hall as she was escorted to the dias where the Sinclair laird and a few of his men stood near the giant fireplace.

No sign of Evan anywhere. Had he been hurt—or worse—in the battle? Mayhap she should have paid better attention to the pile of plaid-draped bodies along the wall in the bailey.

"Ye're asking for me?" The young man beside the laird raised an eyebrow.

Moira quickly stepped back and lowered her gaze away from the man who had ridiculed her along the roadside just a few days ago.

It couldn't be. Yet perhaps she was wrong and Evan wasn't the laird's son after all—or at least not the oldest.

"Well?" His voice conveyed the sneer she imagined spread across his face. "Come to thank me for yer rescue?"

Her naive desire to pursue the marriage alliance fizzled like a fire in the rain for she'd never marry such an oaf and none could force her to do so. There had to be a better way to preserve her clan's future.

"Nay." As Moira scrambled for a reasonable excuse to have approached the man to begin with, her downcast eyes fell on the pouch of herbs strapped to her belt beside the dagger Evan had given her. "I'm a bit of a healer. If ye have any warriors that need tending to I could be of service."

Minutes later, she laid claim to an empty table along one wall. Finella left to fetch her satchel of additional supplies from their hiding place in the woods, and one of the Sinclairs promised to send their wounded to her care.

The first to come for aid was Sheena, the serving girl who'd left Graham's inn searching for a brighter future, and if the rumors were true, had instead met Isla's flying fist not an hour past.

Moira crushed a few herbs and mixed them with water from a nearby cup to create a salve, then applied the remedy to the still-puffy skin covering the girl's cheekbone. "'Twill reduce the swelling and ease the ache."

"Thank ye." Sheena closed her eyes against the pain. "I know ye tried to warn me about her temper, but I wouldn't listen. Today, I couldna let her harm anyone else."

"Ye're a brave one to keep her from poisoning the Sinclairs."

Sheena opened tear-filled eyes. "Nay. Ye're the brave one, M-m-oira. Knowing her as ye did, ye still rallied the clan against her."

Moira glanced around the organized chaos as Isla's body was removed, her guardsmen questioned, and the hall prepared for a celebratory feast that evening. "I should have done it long afore now. But with the help of the Sinclairs, we're finally safe again."

"Safe." Sheena smiled. "Even so, I think I'll be returning to Kilglashan when this is over."

"I almost wish I could do the same." Moira wiped the remaining salve from her fingertips.

The other woman stood. "Nay. Yer rightful place be here, and 'tis my turn to serve ye."

Moira shook her head. "All I need is a basin of hot water and more bandages if ye can find any." She pointed at the first solider approaching with a hand clamped over his upper arm, blood dripping between his fingers. "Appears I'll be here for a while."

Several hours later, she dismissed the last bandaged soldier, straightened her aching back, and put away the remnants of her herbs.

'Twas still no sign of Evan anywhere. While she hoped that meant he'd been uninjured in the fight and was busy assisting others outside the keep, she wasn't ready to face the rows of dead for fear of finding her broken heart among them.

Instead, she had grieving of another sort to do.

Slipping away from the growing crowd and their celebratory mood as the evening's feast was served, she tiptoed up the stairs to the second level and the landing with its view of the great hall.

'Twas odd to witness it all as an outsider. The keep was home…and yet it wasn't.

While the walls displayed the same tapestries she'd walked past a thousand times in her youth, the people she'd loved were missing.

Her father was gone and most of the servants from her childhood had been replaced.

And now Isla was dead, by her own hand. 'Twas belated justice of a sort to hear the rumors that her stepmother had confessed to killing her father.

But that still didn't bring him back.

Seeking to resurrect her memories, Moira turned and headed down the narrow torchlit passage toward the bedchambers.

Near her parents' former chamber, she came upon a rough-hewn table positioned beneath her father's sword mounted upon the wall. She fingered the jeweled hilt, then gazed upon the somewhat shrine-like display of items her father had treasured. The leather belt her mother had commissioned for him early in their marriage. The small silver chest containing the medal awarded his grandfather by

Robert the Bruce after their victory over the English at Bannockburn.

It appeared that Isla might have banished her father's memory from the master bedchamber but displayed the items to convince the Council to support her ongoing role as regent until Roan, as the presumed heir, came of age.

Light from a torch on the wall opposite the display cast flickering shadows over a corner of the table. Atop a folded—and faded—plaid lay Moira's grandmother's wedding brooch—the same intricately carved piece her mother had worn when saying her vows.

Would Moira someday do the same?

The leather cord Moira had worn it on was missing, so with trembling fingers she pinned the sentimental piece to the shoulder of her plaid. Tears welled in her eyes at the familiar weight and the flood of memories. Losing this treasure had hurt almost as much as the damage to her face. Now at least this much had been restored to her.

A scuffing sound on the stone floor caught her attention a moment before the man from her nightmares stepped out of a recessed alcove to her right. In the glow of the closest torch, she was vaguely aware of the ill-fitting yellowish shirt he wore instead of the incriminating red of Isla's guards.

"'Tis a lovely brooch, but ye'll soon wish ye hadn't come to fetch it."

Moira turned and darted for the main stairs, only to be yanked back by Devlin's grip on her dress.

A meaty hand shoved over her mouth cut off her scream. In her periphery, Jenna peeked around the corner of the staircase, then disappeared. For help? To hide?

Moira closed her eyes, and let darkness block out Devlin's face. It didn't matter. No one could help her now.

CHAPTER FOURTEEN

Evan entered the great hall with weary feet and a heavy heart.

After Maggie's—make that Moira's—arrival, he'd slipped out to the bailey to check over the dead and captured Gunn soldiers. While 'twas gratifying to find Toothless and Crooked Nose among the captives and to see their shocked eyes turn fearful at his true identity, Scarface was nowhere to be seen.

Although 'twas possible the captain was roaming the land with another company of traitors. Soldiers who had no idea Isla's reign had ended and might seek to retake the fortress by force.

Knowing the man still lived and could yet cause trouble, Evan walked the ramparts of the walls and spoke to the gatekeepers, ensuring all were on the lookout for Sutherlands and rogue Gunn warriors.

After talking to the cook long enough to determine where the loyalty of the steward lay, he instructed the man to create a listing of those who'd carried out Isla's orders. Once the feasting was over, he vowed to confirm that all of Isla's accomplices were accounted for and brought to justice before he returned to the Sinclair holding.

'Twas at least one last thing he could do for Moira and her people before she married his brother.

The lingering sense of unfinished business did not fully explain the emptiness in his midsection as he once again leaned against the wall near the kitchens.

The parade of fragrant foods nearby could not tempt him to celebrate with the combined clans. Nor the arrival of the last group of Sinclair soldiers escorting Father Tomas and the couple from the inn.

A smile finally cracked his face at the thought of Moira's joy when she realized her parents were safe. Witnessing their reunion would be a memory he'd treasure for the remainder of his lonely days.

That and the stories he'd heard about her recent actions to rally her clan.

Of their own accord, his eyes sought out Moira among the throng but landed instead on one of the girls from the woods.

"Evan." The desperation in Jenna's voice matched the wide-eyed fear on her face. "A man has Moira."

Only one man was unaccounted for. Only one man would be desperate to escape, even to take a hostage...or worse, to finish the job.

He pushed away from the wall. "Where?"

"In the hall upstairs." She pointed back at the main stairs she must have descended.

But those weren't the only stairs that could be used to reach the upper floors.

Jenna's frantic trip across the hall to find him had alerted several of the villagers and loyal Gunn soldiers he'd met while securing the castle. Men who now looked to *him* for guidance.

'Twasn't time for a detailed plan.

With quick gestures, he divided his impromptu company into three groups. "Ye go up the main stairs and ye up the servants' stairs. Cut off those exits and advance slowly. Make enough noise to flush him toward the middle of the hall without startling him into harming her."

The two groups left at a quick jog as he turned to the remaining two men. "Follow me." He led them down the servants' hall toward the kitchen but stopped near a storage room. Nudging the wall and the fringes of his memory, he fumbled for only a moment before activating the lever. A crack appeared in the otherwise ordinary wall.

He hushed the others, then pushed against the panels to fully open the secret door. The dim light from the servants' hall reached far enough inside the opening to reveal a set of narrow stairs…and a discarded red shirt lying at their base.

Proof the man had come this way himself and was now in a disguise of some sort.

He balled the fabric and threw it aside, then met the grim faces of his companions. After whispered instructions for them to guard his flank, he loosened his sword in the sheath at his waist and made his way up the dark stairs with silent footsteps.

Heaven only knew what he'd find when he reached the other side.

Almighty God, protect her from harm and bring justice.

At the top of the stairs, he pressed his ear against the wooden door until he caught the deeper thrum of a man's voice not too far away. With one hand on the hilt of his sword, he inched the door open and slipped into the dark alcove.

As his eyes adjusted to the lighting in the hall, he froze at the sight of the dagger at Moira's neck, the nearby torchlight reflecting off the razor-sharp silver blade. Her captor's attention, however, was distracted as he swiveled his head from side-to-side, monitoring the noisy approach of the other men Evan had sent.

With all escape routes covered, 'twas time to let Moira know help had arrived. Evan braced himself for the fear he was sure he'd find in her eyes.

Except instead of finding her trapped in the pain-filled memories of years gone by, she had closed her eyes and wore an expression of growing acceptance. Just like when she'd faced the charging boar only a week past.

As if she knew her fate was sealed.

* * *

Moira kept her eyes closed as she fought the overwhelming feelings of fear and déjà vu. Devlin's blade wouldna slip this time.

At least she had a few more minutes to live and a few more breaths to draw since he needed her alive as a hostage to get out of the castle. But she wasna fool enough to hope he'd then let her go unscathed.

Except with the sound of heavy footsteps approaching from opposite directions, his plans of escape were likely falling apart. And desperate men often acted rashly.

He adjusted his hold around her midsection, and the metallic scrape of a sword being pulled from a scabbard met her ears. Her eyes flew open to find that Devlin had exchanged his dagger for a sword. As if preparing to fight his way to freedom.

At least there was now an increased distance between her throat and the blade. As the twinge of hope flickered to life, she glanced around the hall, seeking a safe hiding place if given the opportunity.

Her eyes lit upon the shadowed alcove from which Devlin had emerged. The same place where Evan now inched into the light.

She caught her breath. Her hero had once again come to rescue. And since she hadna heard his arrival, the rumors of a secret passage within the castle walls were true.

Evan was alive and unharmed...for now. But his presence so close by could push Devlin over the edge of sanity. She had to get away from the madman.

Moira dug her fingers into the man's arm around her middle, struggling to loosen his hold.

"Let her go." Evan stepped into the full light of the hallway and drew his sword.

Her captor swung them around to face him. "Nay. She's my only way out of here."

"Yer a weakling to hide behind the skirts of a woman." Evan shook his head and took two steps to his right.

With Devlin's attention snared by Evan's deliberate taunts, his left arm had relaxed somewhat, giving her room to draw a full breath. But not enough to slip free.

"Who are ye to care for her? She's a nobody."

The men had circled each other until Devlin's back now faced the alcove.

Evan's gaze shifted to capture hers. "Nay, she's a survivor. A healer."

Joy surged to know how he felt, but now 'twas nothing to stop Devlin from dragging her down the secret passage to make his escape.

Especially when a few loyal Gunn knights and key clan leaders closed in on their position from opposite directions with whispered curses to see her current predicament.

With Devlin penned in on three sides and still holding her captive, why would Evan mention her healing herbs?

The empty pouch still hung at her waist…beside the dagger.

'Twas a message.

She nodded and wiggled again, using her movements to get a hand onto the hilt of her blade.

Evan smiled. "And Moira is the Gunns' natural leader. Her people will follow her anywhere."

Her eyes widened at the realization he now knew her true identity. But the conviction in his words lent her the additional strength she needed to fight for both her heart and her clan. The clan who came to her rescue.

"Did they follow her when they thought she was dead?"

She leaned away from Devlin with just enough pressure that he would believe his arm still held her tightly against his body, but when the opportunity came, there would be room to break free. She eased the dagger from its sheath.

Evan took a step closer. "Aye, they kept her memory alive in their legends. And now ye'll never get away." He nodded to someone or something behind them.

Devlin's quick swivel was all the distraction she needed to slash at his arm, ripping herself free from his grasp at the same time Evan reached for her. She fell into Evan's arms and let him drag her across the hall as her clansmen rushed past them to confront her captor.

Moira dropped the dagger and clung to Evan's broad chest as the clashing of swords behind her ended with a distinctive gurgle, then silence.

Harsh but thorough, justice had been delivered.

Devlin would never harm her again. Her nightmare was finally over.

And she'd been granted another chance to live.

CHAPTER FIFTEEN

Evan sheathed his sword then wrapped both arms around Moira's trembling body.

Over the top of her head, he eyed the bloodied remains of the fiend surrounded by the Gunn leaders who had meted out swift justice on her behalf. He caught the eye of the captain who had followed him up the secret passage. "We need to thoroughly search the castle and grounds—"

"And rout any other cowards who try to hide." The man eyed Evan's hold on their laird's daughter with a slight smile. "Aye. We'll see to the task whilst ye see to her comfort."

The other Gunns exchanged glances and a few nodded his direction. Almost as if they approved of him. Of a match between them.

As the men disappeared down the secret passage taking the body with them, Evan leaned against the stone wall.

'Twas true that he loved this woman with all his heart. And after seeing her face down death for a second time in as many weeks, he wouldna willingly give her over as bride to any other man.

He ran a rough hand over her silky hair, smoothing it away from her face.

Her shaking eased. "Ye came for me after all. I was looking for ye after the battle but must have been mistaken about who ye are."

"Who did ye think me to be, lass?"

She lifted teary eyes. "While ye said ye'd talk to yer da about us, ye never said who he was. And while I never figured a laird would leave his son behind on a hunting trip, back on the road ye were talking to the laird, and I thought ye might be the laird's son, after all. But when I asked for his heir, they took me to that oaf who thinks I'm hideous."

Evan released the breath he'd been holding. She truly had come searching for him. And instead found—

"Donald? He's a pain of an older brother." 'Twas past time to straighten out her confusion. "I am indeed a son of the laird, but as the youngling along on a trip, 'twas easy to forget me."

"I couldna forget ye, Evan Sinclair." Her eyes dipped to his lips and color infused her face.

He brushed a finger along her scar. "And I could never forget ye, even afore I knew ye were truly Moira Gunn."

"I was about to tell ye the truth of who I am." She fingered the antique brooch on her shoulder then glanced down at her feet to retrieve his dagger. "'Twas the same day ye promised to come back for me...and for yer mother's dagger."

She held it out, but he returned it to the sheath at her waist. "Keep it." He lifted her chin and brushed a gentle kiss across her lips. "Mayhap there can be an alliance after all. Wouldna hurt to ask."

"I donna want to marry any but ye. Yet what if my people need..." Her voice trailed off and new tears flooded her beautiful eyes.

His heart clenched to realize how accurate he'd been when he'd guessed at her reasoning. Not only had she been afraid for her personal safety if her identity was known, but she'd also weighed the needs of her clan before her own happiness.

He pressed a finger against Moira's soft lips to silence her fears. "Alliances can be forged without weddings. And with Isla gone, 'tis no reason yer clan must accept the previous terms."

She sighed, then stepped out of his arms. "So we take this one step at a time."

He nodded, then extended an arm to escort her along the hall. "Starting with ye taking yer rightful place in yer clan so ye have a voice in any negotiations."

They made their way back toward the feast below, the sounds of animated conversations echoing the hope bounding throughout him. He couldn't wait to properly introduce her to his father. For her to take her place at the head table among her people.

After all, at a half score and eight, the Gunn's true heir had already shown herself more than capable of rallying their loyalty and support. He smiled. Imagine what she could do while also his wife.

* * *

Moira descended the main stairs to the great hall on Evan's arm.

'Twould have been nice to change into a clean gown before being presented to his father, but she'd sacrificed her only spare for bandages. And she wasna the only Gunn without benefit of finery. 'Twas nothing to be ashamed of considering the events of the day.

At the base of the stairs, she paused to accept a hug from Jenna.

"I'm glad ye're safe. I ken Evan would save ye."

"He wasna alone." She peeked at him. "But I am grateful he was there. God has been gracious to me."

Evan simply nodded, then tugged her forward. They made their way around the tables, a ripple of excitement spreading across the room. Pointing fingers and whispers turned into outbursts of "long live Moira" and wide smiles.

Normally the scrutiny would have made her anxious to hide, but today a warmth spread outward from her heart as the waves of her clan's love—and acceptance—washed over her.

Evan nudged her side and pointed out Graham and Lavena seated at a far table beside Father Tomas. "They are also safe."

"Ye had them brought here?" Tears overflowed from her eyes at the sight of her three closest allies together in one room. Now she could care for them in their older years without fear. And unburden her soul to the priest of her youth.

"Father Tomas was already accompanying my family in their journey here, but after spending hours talking to Graham at the inn while we made our battle plans, he must have made that decision himself."

A few steps later, Dungald halted their progress. Her father's loyal captain spoke to Evan about discovering two more cowards hiding in the cellars. It seemed all of Isla's cohorts were now accounted for.

Evan clapped a strong hand on Dungald's shoulder. "Thank ye for seeing to yer mistress's safety."

A burden she hadn't known she carried lifted from her shoulders. Evan's actions on behalf of her people had not only saved them from Isla's reign of terror but endeared him even further to her heart.

"And I thank ye as well." Moira graced the man with a smile. "My father trusted ye with his life and so do I."

Dungald grimaced. "I didna ken the danger until 'twas too late to save Laird Angus…or ye the first time."

"But yer loyalty never faltered and ye came to our aid today. And for that I am grateful." But it would count for naught if her people did not have a leader to speak on their behalf.

She squeezed Evan's arm beneath her hand. "In the meantime, I need to see what I can do to secure our future."

A future for the two of them and for the rest of the Gunns.

Evan graced her with a warm smile, then led her to the head table, stopping near where the Sinclair laird and his oafish son Donald had already claimed seats. The same carved chairs where her own father and mother—and later Isla—used to sit during meals.

"Father, may I present Moira, the daughter of the previous laird, Angus Gunn."

Moira kept her chin up and gaze focused on Evan's father, ignoring the inevitable stares of the nearby Sinclair men. They'd seen her by the roadside before, but would they believe her now?

Evan rested his free hand atop hers and squeezed. "After Isla's original attempt on her life failed, Graham—the innkeeper ye met a few days ago— rescued her, and she's been living in hiding under an assumed name. Having reached her majority, her existence nullifies any claim Isla made to clan leadership."

The questioning gazes eased into nods of respect. Mayhap because of the tale Evan told...or mayhap because of the whispered stories already circulating through the hall.

The Sinclair laird frowned. "How came ye by yer injuries?"

The hall quieted and she took a deep breath. Better to answer the questions once than over and over.

"Over five years ago, while my father lay dying, I escaped to the woods for a bit of privacy to grieve. One of the soldiers Isla brought with her when she married my father followed me there. Ripped away the necklace holding my mother's brooch." She fingered the thin mark around her neck, and then traced the rough scar leading up to her temple. "Placed his blade to my neck, but it went awry when my knees buckled. I evaded his pursuit when I fell into the ravine."

"And why did ye stay away for so long?"

She darted a glance to the table where Graham and his beloved wife sat. "I almost died from blood loss and an infection, but by the time I'd recovered, my father was dead and the council had appointed Isla as regent until Roan came of age. I was but a half score and three and didna ken who to trust. I feared Isla would finish the task herself and also harm those who sheltered me. 'Twas safer to let the rumors of my death linger."

She swallowed hard. "I regret not coming forward after Roan's death, but I still feared Isla's retribution. By the time I too was of age, staying hidden was a hard habit to break." A quick glance at Evan bolstered her courage. "Until I met yer son and began to stand up for others who'd been mistreated. His actions reminded me of my duty to the rest of my people and gave me the courage to step forward."

Evan's father nodded, then motioned for two of his soldiers to give up their seats for her and Evan.

As she took the place near where her mother had always sat, other conversations around the hall resumed. One of the castle servants brought her and Evan a fresh trencher of food to share and she dug into the delicacies. It had been hours since her meager portion of porridge around a campfire that morn.

Her hunger had barely been appeased when the Sinclair laird resumed his questioning. "I've heard ye were in the woods today with those who cut off the escape of some, but where have ye been hiding since then?" His stern gaze flickered from her to his son and back again.

Surely he didna think...

Heat rose in her face at the implications. "I spent several hours stitching up yer wounded men right over there in plain sight." She pointed to the far side of the hall, then at a few of the bandaged men nearby who could verify her actions. "Afterward I took a walk upstairs to revisit my childhood home. And that's where Evan came to my rescue...again."

"Again?" His eyebrows rose as if doubting her word. Or doubting his son's abilities as a warrior.

She raised her voice. "Yes, again. Over the past sennight, yer son faced down and distracted Isla's soldiers at the inn to protect two village lasses he hadna met before. He then helped us to escape through the woods and was injured while killing a wild boar two feet afore it ran me through."

The hall had grown silent again, but she didna care who overheard her words so long as the laird comprehended his second son's bravery. "He protected me from those same soldiers who came to drag me back to Isla, found us a new hiding place, and built a shelter for even more of the displaced lasses despite battling his own injury."

She drew in a deep breath as the memories came flooding back and turned her attention to the red-faced man beside her. Both clans needed to know what a hero he was.

"And just now upstairs he led the charge to rescue me from the same man who tried once before to murder me." She rested a hand on Evan's arm, then refocused on the Sinclair laird's stunned face. "Ye needn't look so shocked. Yer son is a true hero."

* * *

Evan squirmed on the wooden bench.

Being the center of attention wasn't as wonderful as he'd once hoped. Although nothing Moira had said was untrue, hearing it all in one tale in front of his clan—and hers— he wished they were alone in the woods again.

He risked a glance at his father's face to find a look of respect lingering there.

His brother grunted as Moira's tale ended. "Ye left out the part where he saved us too."

"'Tis the truth." His father nodded, then turned his attention to Evan. "Ye warned us about Isla's actions and the possibility of a double-cross with the Sutherlands. I hadn't taken ye seriously afore, but yer methods to recruit the servants while warning us to use caution saved us from being poisoned as well."

A cheer rose from several people around the hall with still more shouting his name as a hero.

Heat rushed to his face.

His father stood and raised a cup of ale. "A toast to the safe return of Moira Gunn as the rightful leader of Clan Gunn." A resounding cheer echoed off the stone walls as both clans celebrated the woman beside him.

Once the cheers died down, his father cleared his throat. "Moira, if ye be in favor of forging a new alliance between our clans while this time retaining yer clan's lands and name, I offer Evan as the son worthy to live at and protect Castle Gunn."

His heart in his throat, Evan snapped his attention to the lovely woman beside him. To have her hand in marriage. To build a family together. And to have a holding of his own to manage.

'Twas a dream come true for him. And if it meant giving up his home by the sea or even his name, she was worth the sacrifice.

But what about her?

He held his breath as she turned glowing eyes his direction with a shy smile. She stood and lifted her own cup. "If my clan agrees, I am in favor of such an alliance."

From his place two tables away, Dungald stood. "All in favor of a marriage between our Moira and Evan Sinclair?"

The ayes echoed off the walls.

Moira tapped her goblet of ale against his father's to seal the informal deal.

With murmurs of excitement about an upcoming wedding and a formal alliance rippling throughout the room around them, Moira turned to face him.

Evan rose to his feet beside her. "Are ye sure?" He searched her eyes for any lingering doubts.

"Aye." A blush tinged her face but love shone from her eyes.

He lowered his voice so only she could hear. "I vow to always cherish and protect ye...and yer people."

She lifted a hand to cup the side of his face. "Me da would have loved ye…as I do."

"But not as much as I love ye." Evan followed his ardent declaration with a lingering kiss, then reluctantly pulled away.

A moment later, with hands intertwined, they faced their people and stepped into the light of their future.

* * * * *

DEAR READER

I've always loved fairy tales and as a girl, dreamed of someday living in a castle and meeting my very own Prince Charming. As I grew, those romantic notions shifted to include a love for stories set in the Scottish Highlands and Regency England until the mountain of books I read translated into new characters roaming throughout my imagination.

And so was born this newest series which will eventually include four historical tales and a contemporary novel that ties them all together.

While I am not physically scarred like Moira or overlooked like Evan, there have been times where I've felt insignificant and content to linger in the shadows while others took the limelight. And yet, hiding away only denied the unique gifts the Creator bestowed and kept me from living out my true identity as a daughter of the King.

Writing a story set in the medieval Scottish Highlands involved a lot of research to get as many details correct as I could. While I know mistakes are likely, I hope they did not detract from Moira and Evan's adventures. Special thanks goes out to my critique partner Laura Hilton for wading into a new genre with me and to my editor Marisa Deshaies for helping me to clarify the confusing parts.

If you think other readers would enjoy this story, please do me a huge favor and leave an honest review at Goodreads, Amazon, and other retailers. A review doesn't have to be more than a few words, but means so much to me!

Speaking of reviews, if you'd like to be a part of my official reviewer team with advance access to upcoming releases, email me at Candee@CandeeFick.com and I'll send you the link to sign up. Or if you'd rather just receive my monthly newsletter including information about upcoming releases, you can sign up using the form on my website at www.CandeeFick.com.

Thanks again for spending time with one of my books. Happy reading everyone!

MORE BOOKS BY CANDEE FICK

<u>Standalone Fiction</u>

Catch of a Lifetime

<u>The Wardrobe Series</u>

Dance Over Me
Focus On Love
Sing a New Song (available May 2019)
A Picture Perfect Christmas
Home For Christmas (coming November 2019)

<u>Within the Castle Gates</u>

Stepping Into the Light
To Win Her Heart (coming Spring 2019)
The Lost Heir (TBD)
Finding Home (TBD)
Saving Grace (TBD)

<u>Non-Fiction</u>

The Author Toolbox: Practical Tools to Build a Book, a
Platform, a Business, and a Career
Pigskin Parables: Exploring Faith and Football
Pigskin Parables: Devotions from the Game of Football
Making Lemonade: Parents Transforming Special Needs
Devotions from the Garden: Inspiration for Life
Be Like a Tree: The Keys to a Fruitful Life

PREVIEW
TO WIN HER HEART

Within the Castle Gates series, Book 2
Releasing Spring 2019

A deathbed promise puts one man at odds with the desire of
his heart...
while one woman's duty to family may cost her everything
she'd ever dreamed of.

Despite Emma Richards' fanciful dreams growing up in the
shadow of King Arthur's castle and the manor on the cliff,
the orphan is now trapped inland serving her wealthy cousins
with no hope for her own future.

Sir Grayson Wentworth spent his years at Cambridge
dreaming of the Cornwall coast and wishing he could return
to the happy days of his youth. Called home to his father's
deathbed, the young lord soon learns he has inherited a title, a
neglected estate, and a betrothal agreement he knew nothing
about.

When the new Baron Danvers travels to execute the last
matters of his father's will, he finds himself promised to one
woman and falling for another. Can he keep his vow to find a
wife and win her heart? Or will honor be sacrificed in the
name of love?

~March 1750; along the Cornwall coast

Grayson Wentworth dismounted from the hired carriage
with stiff muscles and an uncomfortable sense of
foreboding.

Over the past three days journeying from Cambridge, the initial reluctance to leave his studies incomplete so close to the commencement ceremonies had been pushed aside by the exhilarating knowledge that, after seven years preparing to embrace his role as a future peer of the realm, he'd finally been summoned back to Wentworth Manor.

After stepping away from the panting horses, Grayson swiveled toward the arched openings in the high stone wall and inhaled the salty air that was rich with bittersweet memories and the smell of decaying fish rising from the seaside village of Danvers nestled among the rugged cliffs below.

No matter the reality awaiting inside, the familiar panoramic view from above the tiny harbor lifted his spirits. Even Cambridge with all the expected pomp of nobility and the weight of vaulted academia could not compete with the wild beauty of his birthplace.

There was no place he'd rather be.

If only his homecoming wasn't tainted by the report of his father's illness. The mere fact Baron Danvers had admitted a weakness only heightened his trepidation.

Grayson turned toward the imposing yet regal structure perched like a castle above the commoners. But unlike the impressive buildings he'd left behind, this one wore a cloak of neglect. His gaze swept over the dingy window panes, faded whitewash, and dead foliage lingering around the foundation.

With winter's worst behind them, the tasks should have at least been in progress by now. During his childhood, the Lenten season was spent preparing the heart to celebrate the resurrection…and preparing the manor house and surrounding fields for spring.

In fact, along the road from Boscastle toward Danvers, he'd spied a number of plowed fields readied for planting. Was the local delay a matter of money? Of time? Or the result of lazy servants without proper supervision?

A knot formed in his stomach. Something was definitely wrong and seemed to have been so for quite some time. Long before the brief letter bearing his father's seal had been dispatched to the university.

Grayson took a deep breath of courage before striding across the weed-infested cobblestones of the courtyard. Halfway up the leaf-littered exterior staircase, the front door burst open and a tardy footman bounded down the steps, proof that the household was in residence even if lax in their duties.

The errant employee paused a moment. "I'll fetch your baggage to your rooms Master Grayson, er, Sir."

Grayson brushed aside the alarm that he wasn't a Sir anything...yet, then with a quick nod at the young man, continued his way toward the entrance.

After crossing the threshold, he eyed the empty foyer with its mixture of polished woodwork and marble floor. The space was unchanged from his youth, including the grand staircase with the smooth banisters he'd attempted to slide down long before being shipped off to school.

Everything was as he'd remembered, except for the conspicuous absence of their butler.

Where was everyone?

A week had passed since the message was sent, so would he find his father abed or in his study?

Grayson headed down the wide passage to the left of the main staircase, but stopped at a creaking noise overhead and retraced his steps.

"Master Grayson?"

Like the previous footman, their longtime butler had finally made an appearance.

"Miles." Grayson met the silver-haired gentleman at the foot of the stairs. "At last, a familiar face to welcome me home." However, the years had taken their toll and it was hard to reconcile his memories with the gaunt and stooped man before him.

The butler's smile widened as he inventoried the changes in Grayson's frame. After all, he'd left a boy and had returned a man. "The years have been good to you, lad." His smile faded. "You're needed above." Miles pointed in the direction of the baron's bedchamber. "He did not wish to disturb your studies until it was absolutely necessary."

Grayson nodded, then headed up the grand staircase.

He'd been begging to come home for years, but had agreed to further advanced studies only to keep his father happy. But no more. As a grown man, he'd fight to stay at the manor, a place where he was obviously needed.

At the top of the stairs, he glanced to his right toward the wing housing his childhood rooms and others for guests. Time enough to settle in later.

Grayson instead turned left toward his parents' suite and his late mother's private drawing room. The somewhat-threadbare rugs in the lavish hall muffled his steps, but the limited supply of candles reminded him again of the general sense of neglect he'd observed outside.

He needed to question their steward and examine the books so he could get to work fixing the problem. But maintaining their property would have to wait because the estate's biggest problem lay down the hall.

Grayson paused at the entrance to the baron's bedroom. The door was ajar, but he knocked anyway out of habit. Not to mention the fact that after such a long absence, he felt like a stranger in his own home.

A cough, and then a weak voice. "Enter."

Grayson nudged his way into the darkened room where a fire blazed on the hearth.

"Welcome home, son." Baron Danvers' once forceful voice had been reduced to a mere whisper.

After swallowing the lump of emotion in his throat, Grayson quickly crossed to his father's side where he lay on the enormous four-postered bed. "I left the morning after your letter arrived. You should have sent for me sooner."

A frail hand lifted from the blankets to wave away his comments.

The baron's faithful valet rose from a chair beside the bed and gestured for Grayson to take the seat.

"What happened?" Grayson's voice cracked and he fought to hide his horror at how his once robust sire had faded to a shriveled form buried beneath a mountain of blankets in the already sweltering room.

The valet glanced at his employer, then cleared his throat. "Months ago, the baron's new horse spooked and threw him to the ground, then trampled him. The physician said there were internal injuries in addition to his broken leg."

Grayson sank onto the padded chair as the faithful servant described the long journey through various infections and fevers. But just as his father seemed to be recovering, consumption had settled in his lungs. Despite his already-weakened condition and poor prognosis, the Baron had still spent a fortune on doctors seeking a cure.

And since the estate's staff had been reduced as a result of their financial situation, there were now too many tasks spread among too few people.

"We need...your help. But...I'm sorry...to cut short...your education." His father's whispered apology ended in a violent coughing fit. The valet hurried to assist the baron into an upright position before propping more pillows behind him.

"I've learned enough." While the words were meant to soothe, they were also true. While meeting with his advising professor to explain his hasty departure, Grayson had learned that with the exception of one last academic paper that could be submitted via courier, the rest of his marks were sufficient to graduate at the end of the term.

He would have been returning home in a few months regardless. And yet, all of those years at Cambridge had taken him away from his father's side. He'd been seated in a classroom instead of observing the inner workings of the estate and building ties with the villagers.

Finally done coughing, the baron collapsed back against the pillows and wiped a handkerchief across his lips. The white linen came away stained with bloody phlegm.

Grayson's heart clenched. All those years he could have spent with his sole remaining family member instead of arriving home only to bury his father.

There would be no new life this Easter season, only another grave.

Until the inevitable happened, however, he vowed to ease his father's suffering and make every moment count.

The normally stern visage of the baron had melted into that of a broken man. "Take care...of the place...your mother...loved it so."

Swallowing the lump in his throat at the childhood memories of his mother, Grayson gently squeezed his father's hand. "I will."

"Won't be here...to guide you." Another whisper, followed by a frown.

As if he worried his son would not be able to run the estate without guidance.

As if his heir was unfit.

Grayson fought the urge to retreat to the study to examine their accounts before touring the estate. Once armed with information, he could better ease his father's worries. And yet, his years of education were not in vain. "I know what to do. Between my boyhood memories and Cambridge, I'm prepared. And if I have any questions, I can always ask the steward or Miles. In the meantime, you need to rest."

The exhausted baron nodded, then relaxed deeper into the pillows. "One more...thing...and I...can be...at peace."

Based on the gray cast to his father's skin, the end was near. In a sudden rush of emotion, all Grayson's past hurts were replaced by the keen desire to please his father once again.

"Anything."

"Promise...me." The ghost of a smile flitted across his father's gaunt face. "Find a wife."

At Cambridge, he'd suffered numerous encounters with matchmaking mothers and their vapid daughters, making a wife the last thing on his mind. And yet, he would need to marry eventually to produce an heir.

"I will." Agreement came easily since it bore no timetable.

"Find a wife…and win her heart."

A neglected longing stirred within.

Maybe someday this cold home would once again ring with laughter and music like when his mother had lived.

ABOUT THE AUTHOR

Candee Fick is a romance editor for a small Christian press and a multi-published award-winning author. She is the wife of a high school football coach and the mother of three children, including a daughter with a rare genetic syndrome. When not busy editing or writing, she can be found cheering on the home team at sporting events, exploring the great Colorado outdoors, indulging in dark chocolate, and savoring happily-ever-after endings through a good book.

In addition to writing clean faith-based romance novels and inspirational non-fiction, Candee coaches other authors with their marketing plans and offers content editing to aspiring novelists. She is a member of both American Christian Fiction Writers (ACFW) and the Christian Proofreaders and Editors Network. Her fiction has semi-finaled, finaled, and won the ACFW Genesis Contest and Selah Awards.

Visit her website: https://CandeeFick.com

Made in the USA
Coppell, TX
03 April 2020